PREYED UPON

DENISE N. WHEATLEY

Harlequin

INTRIGUE

To my mother, Donna, my forever partner in crime...

Harlequin®
INTRIGUE™

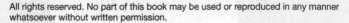

ISBN-13: 978-1-335-45749-3

Preyed Upon

Copyright © 2025 by Denise N. Wheatley

Recycling programs
for this product may
not exist in your area.

 Harlequin Enterprises ULC
22 Adelaide St. West, 41st Floor
Toronto, Ontario M5H 4E3, Canada
www.Harlequin.com

Printed in Lithuania

MIX
Paper | Supporting
responsible forestry
FSC® C021394

Denise N. Wheatley loves happy endings and the art of storytelling. Her novels run the romance gamut, and she strives to pen entertaining books that embody matters of the heart. She's an RWA member and holds a BA in English from the University of Illinois. When Denise isn't writing, she enjoys watching true crime TV and chatting with readers. Follow her on social media.

Instagram: @Denise_Wheatley_Writer
X: @DeniseWheatley
BookBub: @DeniseNWheatley
Goodreads: Denise N. Wheatley

Books by Denise N. Wheatley

Harlequin Intrigue

A West Coast Crime Story

The Heart-Shaped Murders
Danger in the Nevada Desert
Homicide at Vincent Vineyard
Hometown Homicide
Preyed Upon

An Unsolved Mystery Book

Cold Case True Crime

Bayou Christmas Disappearance
Backcountry Cover-Up

Harlequin Medical Romance

ER Doc's Las Vegas Reunion

Visit the Author Profile page at Harlequin.com.

CAST OF CHARACTERS

Chloe Grant—A former Chicago police detective turned true crime podcaster who has returned to her hometown of Maxwell, Arizona.

Troy Miller—A childhood friend of Chloe's who now works for the Maxwell PD.

Danielle (Dani) Miller—Troy's older sister and Maxwell's chief of police.

Alex Harrison—Chloe's ex-boyfriend who works as an attorney in Chicago.

Melissa Chaney—Alex's new girlfriend.

Justin Walters—A Chicago police detective who once worked side by side with Chloe.

Simon Grazer—Head writer on the police drama television series *The Chicago Force*.

Gretchen Knight—The number one fan of Chloe's true crime podcast.

Prologue

Detective Chloe Grant parked her unmarked car near the end of the block and turned to her partner. "You know the plan, right?"

"I know the plan," Detective Justin Walters confirmed, tightening the shoulder strap on his bulletproof vest. "You got the warrant?"

"Yes, I have it."

Chloe eyed the run-down exterior of the Righteous Nation's headquarters—home of Chicago's most notorious gang. Harsh winters had eaten away at the wooden two-flat's black exterior. Rotting window frames bordered foggy, cracked panes. Crumbling cement stairs led to a rusted wrought iron door. The building, once owned by a member's grandmother, had seen better days. It'd become quite an eyesore among the Craftsman bungalows lining the street, appearing more like a haunted house than a well-kept home.

"The other officers have already made their way inside," Chloe told Justin, grabbing her door handle. "We'll go in behind them and—"

"Wait," he interrupted. "Before we kick this off, can I ask you something?"

Chloe's stomach lurched at the question. *Now is not the time*, she wanted to say. "Sure," she replied instead.

"Your, uh…your next meeting with Internal Affairs is tomorrow. Right?"

Here we go…

"Yes. It is."

"And you know they're gonna press you about the money that went missing the night we took down the Reckless Assassins."

Chloe nodded, bracing herself for what was coming.

"You don't really believe that I stole it, do you?"

Silence.

"*Do* you?"

"Justin," Chloe croaked, her mouth drying out as if she'd swallowed a spoonful of sand. "I cannot have this conversation with you right now. Let's just focus on the investigation at hand. The other officers are waiting on us."

She swung open the door and stepped out of the car. He didn't budge.

"Detective Walters, let's move."

"No. Not until you tell me you'll have my back at that meeting tomorrow."

Chloe's head fell against the door frame. "Look, if I'm being honest, I do think it's strange how that money went missing. I counted it myself before handing the bag over to you."

"Right, but maybe you miscounted—"

"I counted $200,000 exactly," Chloe interrupted, heat rising up her neck at the accusation. "*Several* times. Yet once the bag made it to the evidence room, there was only $80,000. And you were never able to explain why."

"Detective Grant, that crime scene was hectic as hell. There was a ton of evidence that needed to be collected. My guess is that the money got lost in the shuffle. Plus, you *know* me. You know I wouldn't have stolen that money. Like I was saying, you must've miscounted it."

"And like *I* was saying, that absolutely didn't happen!"

Memories of that night flickered through Chloe's head. Cops storming the run-down drug house. Suspects scattering in every direction. Flashlights beaming and bullets flying. Loud commands bouncing off the dingy walls. The scene had been chaotic. Yet Chloe had remained on high alert, keeping close tabs on everything happening around her. She was positive that Justin's hands were the last to touch that bag of money.

"Detective Walters," Chloe continued while readjusting her holster, "we've gotta get inside. A lot of planning went into this sting operation. I'd hate for it to go left—"

"Just give me your word that you'll tell Internal Affairs I didn't take that money."

She responded by slamming the door and heading up the block.

"Officer Daniels," Chloe said into her Bluetooth microphone, "has the squad made it through the house yet?"

"Not all the way through, but we're getting there. We've got two officers on the upper level and three on the main floor. So far, the place looks pretty empty."

"Any sightings of drugs or weapons?"

"No. But trust me, we're scouring this place from top to bottom."

"Good." Chloe turned to make sure Justin had gotten out of the car. She was relieved to see him following closely behind. "Detective Walters and I are making our way inside the backyard now."

"Ten-four."

The detectives trampled through a maze of rusted-out

junk cars, barbecue grills and trash cans before entering the basement through a dry-rotted door.

"Let's split up," Justin said. "I'll go check out the attic while you look around down here."

"Wait. That's not what we discussed—"

Before Chloe could finish, Justin shot up the stairs, leaving her alone inside the dank lower level.

"All righty, then."

She sucked in a sharp inhalation, almost gagging on the putrid stench of urine and burned plastic. Pulling a flashlight from her belt, Chloe scanned the grimy, dimly lit area. Dusty black garbage bags shielded the windows. Trails of dirty shoe prints lined the uneven vinyl floors. A few dingy white folding chairs were scattered about. Syringes, cold medications and pill bottles covered dented steel tables. Most alarming were the droplets of blood splattered against the peeling drywall.

Chloe surveyed the walls with her Glock 22 drawn, peering around every shadowy corner. The area appeared empty. And the contraband law enforcement had hoped to find was nowhere in sight.

"All clear down in the basement," Chloe whispered into her mic. "Anything on the upper floors?"

The question was met with silence.

"Detective Walters? Come in, Detective Walters."

Still nothing.

"Officer Daniels? Somebody…talk to me."

All static. No response.

Chloe headed toward the landing just as unfamiliar voices boomed through the stairwell. She froze.

Those aren't my officers.

Charging toward the other side of the room, she crouched

behind a tattered couch. The cracked leather scratched her cheek on the way down.

"Damn it!" Chloe uttered, the sting snaking across her jawline.

She gripped the lapel on her black blazer and hissed into the mic, "Detective Walters! I'm still in the basement, and it sounds like we've got company. I need the entire squad down here, *ASAP*."

Chloe held her breath while awaiting a reply. Nothing but dead air poured through the earpiece.

She rose a few inches and peered over the sofa. For a brief moment, everything blurred. Panic festered in the pit of Chloe's gut as she realized she'd been left to fend for herself during the biggest bust of her career—the culmination of an operation she'd been heading up for months.

Heavy footsteps pounded the rickety wooden staircase. Craning her neck, Chloe watched as three burly men dressed in dark jogging suits paraded into the room. They were easily recognizable. Rocko, Boris and June. The leaders of the Righteous Nation.

They'd been under police surveillance for over a year. The department was on a mission to take them down on a slew of charges, from drug trafficking and kidnapping to firearm possession and fraud. Tonight was the night. But Chloe knew they were heavily armed and highly dangerous. There was no way she could move in on them alone.

Sweat trickled down her temples as tendrils of jet-black curls stuck to the sides of her slender face. Her burning ears pricked up when the men's phones rang in unison. Each shrill tone jabbed at her head, causing a migraine to peak at full speed.

"Look," one of them said, "enough with the phones. Ignore the calls and get to work. Our schedule is tight, and we can't afford to make any mistakes this time."

They shuffled past the couch carrying large black duffel bags. June's was slightly unzipped. Chloe caught sight of several bricks of cocaine stacked inside.

A burst of adrenaline detonated inside her chest. She had never been this close to taking them down. The thought of finally apprehending the elusive gang members almost sent her leaping over the couch. But she fought the urge. It was too risky considering the unit had yet to show up.

Suddenly, it registered why. Justin and the rest of the squad were rallying against her. Trying to teach her a lesson after she'd refused to lie for him.

Chloe hated that she didn't believe Justin's story. They'd worked together for five of the eight years she had served on the force and formed a solid bond. At some point, Justin had become less like a colleague and more like a friend.

But she had taken an oath of honor. So regardless of their relationship, that promise left her no choice but to stick to the truth and not change the facts on her report about the money.

While Justin's future with the Chicago PD remained to be seen, all she could think of was how he'd left her alone to confront three of Chicago's most ruthless gangsters.

"Hey, Rocko!" she heard one of them yell. "We got everything we need for the drop?"

"What?"

"Man, stop looking at the phone and pay attention! I said, do we have everything we need for the drop?"

"I don't know, June!"

"Well, grab a couple extra bricks just in case. And make it quick. It's time to go. We're *really* pressed for time now."

Chloe took a deep breath. Reality set in as she realized she might have to take the men down by herself. The alternative—

aborting the mission—was not an option. Not after all the intense strategizing she had done. Finishing what she'd started was a must.

Chloe increased the volume on her earpiece and listened for the sound of voices, movement, anything that would indicate her unit was on the way down. She was met with complete silence.

"We good?" June asked.

"Yep, we good," Rocko confirmed. "Let's make a move."

Chloe gritted her teeth as panic set in. The men were preparing to leave. She couldn't let that happen.

Tightening her grip on her gun, she duckwalked toward the edge of the couch. Stayed low and pivoted. Just as she turned the corner, her combat boot hit the steel leg.

"Hold on," one of the men said. "What the hell was that?"

"What the hell was what?"

"I heard some noise coming from the corner."

Damn it!

Chloe's calf muscles quivered as her finger hugged the trigger. She braced herself while shoe soles screeched across the floor, then stooped lower when they grew closer.

"Hey! Who's in here?"

Holding her breath, Chloe prepared to jump to her feet. But her legs failed to launch.

The operation suddenly felt more like a suicide mission. Never had she imagined having to face the notorious gang members without her team. Instinct was telling her to stay put. Years on the force had taught her to never go against her gut. So she remained rooted behind the couch.

"Come on, man," a voice grumbled right above Chloe's head. "There's nobody down here but us. Now, let's get back to what we were—"

Footsteps clamored overhead, cutting him off.

Please be my team...

"There may not be anybody down here," Rocko uttered. "But clearly there's somebody upstairs. Who was supposed to meet us, Boris?"

"Nobody. But best believe if somebody had the audacity to walk in here uninvited, they won't be walking out alive. Aye, grab that AK-47!"

The guttural rasp in his tone sent a subzero chill straight through Chloe. She'd warned the unit that their suspects might be armed. But these men were ready for war.

The click of magazines being shoved into guns rattled as the basement door swung open. Peering over the couch, Chloe watched as all three men aimed their weapons toward the landing.

"Don't ask no questions," Boris said. "Soon as you see a body? Start shooting."

Just as their fingers rounded the triggers, someone yelled, "Hey, Rocko! You down there?"

The men's guns fell by their sides.

"Damn it, Deuce! You almost got your head blown off. Why didn't you tell us you were gonna be here?"

Chloe couldn't make out his rambling response. Her eardrums were ringing with dread. The unit had failed her. She might not come out of this alive.

The room suddenly grew excruciatingly hot as everything around her darkened. Chloe rocked back on her aching feet, then fell against the wall.

"Wait," one of the men huffed. "What was that?"

Feet shuffled in her direction. There was nowhere to hide. It was four against one.

Brace yourself, Chloe thought right before the couch flipped over.

Rocko's steely eyes, burrowed deep within his drawn, tattooed face, bore down on her.

"Police!" she yelled, raising her gun while scrambling to her feet. "Stand down and drop your weapons. All of you!"

The men turned to one another, each doubling over with laughter like a row of falling dominoes.

"Is she serious?" June asked, running his tongue along his gapped teeth.

"I said, stand down, now!" Chloe repeated, pointing her gun at June.

Bang! Bang! Bang!

She dropped to her knees as a hail of bullets whizzed past her head. None of them hit. But the warning was clear.

"No, bitch," Boris rebutted. "*You* stand down. Unless you wanna lose your life."

Outnumbered and abandoned, Chloe struggled to figure out her next move. Nothing seemed feasible. But if she didn't do something, she'd be killed.

Rocko nudged June's shoulder. "Man, just tie her up and throw her in my trunk. We'll deal with her after we make this drop."

Do something! the voice inside Chloe's head cried out.

She looked on in agony as June grabbed a bundle of tattered cable wires. Expecting backup was a lost cause. But there was no way in hell Chloe would allow herself to be tied up, stuffed inside a trunk and taken who knew where.

I'd rather die right here...

Boom!

Shooting pain exploded inside Chloe's head. She fell to the floor, gripping the side of her face. Her skull felt as though it'd been shattered into a thousand little pieces. Had she been shot? Hit with a fist, or the butt of a gun?

One of the men approached from behind and snatched her

weapon. His cohort pulled her arms behind her back and tied a cord around her wrists.

Chloe struggled to open her eyes. The blow had weakened her vision as well as her will. As her thumping heartbeat slowed, the effort to fill her heaving chest with air drained every ounce of energy.

Don't give up. Don't give up...

Steel poked through the wires restraining her hands. The shards of metal cut into her skin. She emitted a low moan. It couldn't be heard over the men's barrage of banter. They were thrilled with Chloe's capture.

Fight back! she told herself. But she couldn't. She was fading.

Another round of footsteps clambered overhead. Just as she felt herself blacking out, Chloe finally heard the one word she'd been waiting on...

"Police!"

Chapter One

Officer Troy Miller strolled through the Maxwell police station, a turkey on rye in one hand and police report in the other.

"How'd it go, Miller?"

He tossed Natalia a thumbs-up, squinting at the sight of the receptionist's lavender bob. Yesterday her hair had been in waist-length platinum braids. But the former model–turned–Maxwell PD desk clerk had recently launched a YouTube channel, declaring she'd be the biggest beauty influencer in all of Arizona by the end of the year. The ever-changing looks were a part of the job and something Troy was still getting used to.

"It went as well as I'd expected," he told her.

"Meaning Mr. Diaz's house hadn't really been broken into?"

"No, it had not. Just like it hadn't been last week, or the week before. I did have a talk with his sister before I left. She's in denial about his dementia and doesn't believe it's getting worse. After thirty minutes of back-and-forth, I finally convinced her to make an appointment with a specialist."

"Good. Look at you, Officer Miller. Law enforcement needs more policemen like you out here helping the people."

"Thanks, Natalia. Just doing my job."

He held back the part where the job was a far cry from the type of work he really wanted to be doing.

After attending the University of Southern California on a swimming scholarship, the six-foot-three athlete had set major goals for himself that included competing in the Olympics and coaching a Division I swim team. But during his sophomore year, a lower back injury thwarted his plans. He'd developed a love-hate relationship with swimming that leaned more toward hate. It had gotten so bad that the sight of a pool or scent of chlorine turned his stomach.

Troy had almost dropped out of school, but then he'd met Lena Love, an aspiring criminalist who came from a family of law enforcement officers. They had that in common, as, back then, his father was Maxwell's chief of police and his older sister was destined to become an officer. Troy's relationship with Lena inspired him to switch his major from exercise science to emergency medicine services.

After graduation, both he and Lena accepted jobs with the LAPD—him as a paramedic and her as a forensic scientist. But when she was viciously attacked by a serial killer, Lena moved back to her hometown of Clemmington, California. Shortly thereafter, Troy found out that his father was retiring from the force and his sister, Danielle, fondly known as Dani, was taking over as chief of police. So he returned to Maxwell and entered the police department's training academy in support of his family.

Troy had thought the career switch would generate a deeper level of intention and purpose. Problem was, he'd forgotten that he was going from the thrilling city of LA, where everything moved at a frenzied pace, to Maxwell, population a little over six thousand, where the slower pace was a way of life.

"Hey, Troy! Is that you I hear out there?"

He rolled his eyes at the sound of Dani's voice booming

from her office. He'd asked her time and time again to refer to him as Officer Miller when they were at work.

"Yeah, okay, T-Rex," she'd replied after the first request, referencing a childhood nickname sparked by Troy's obsession with dinosaurs. The mention of it drummed up memories of his youth, back when their five-year age difference had her in a constant state of teasing.

"Please do not call me that," he'd told her. "Especially here at the station."

The last thing Troy needed was for the veteran cops to catch wind of his youthful moniker. It would undoubtedly send their lighthearted hazing of the neophyte officers into overdrive.

"Are you coming?" Dani called out, sounding as though she'd moved from behind her desk toward the hallway.

"Yes, I am, Chief Miller!"

On the way to her office, Troy pulled in a puff of air and glanced around the station. The metallic scent of fresh paint still lingered in the air, as the walls had recently been spruced up with a soft shade of blue. The newly laid beige terrazzo flooring, cherrywood standing desks and comfy ergonomic chairs were all extras that Dani had added to boost the look of the department as well as employee morale.

Troy hovered in her doorway, watching as she wiped down the keyboard with a disinfecting cloth. Being a neat freak, workaholic and self-proclaimed germophobe were just a few of the traits she prided herself on.

"Come on in and have a seat," Dani said. "Tell me how things went with Mr. Diaz." She looked up from her desk, her wide-set hazel eyes homing in on the top of Troy's freshly cut hair and moving down to his face. "How was your day? Are you okay?"

He set his lunch on the desk and took a seat, letting off a low grunt on the way down. "I'm good. But my quads are on

fire from last night's spin class. As for Mr. Diaz, you probably overheard me telling Natalia that the majority of my visit
was spent discussing his dementia diagnosis with his sister.
After that, I patrolled the streets a bit. Nothing happening
there. Now I'm back. I've been on the clock since six this
morning, so I'll be off soon. I'll probably finish up a couple
of impound reports before I head out…"

Troy's voice trailed off as his eyes drifted toward a framed
photo hanging on Dani's wall. It had been taken a couple of
years ago at Cole's Ski Resort—one of Maxwell's main tour-
ist attractions. The resort, the charming old-fashioned downtown and various holistic wellness spas were huge draws
for visitors.

The town's high altitude meant tourists could come enjoy
some of the best skiing, snowboarding and tubing experiences Arizona had to offer during the winter. Eighteen-hole
golf games and scenic mountain hikes filled the summer
months. The resort was a premier destination, even for the
locals. Troy went there whenever he wanted to impress a
date—a fact he was reminded of every time he saw that
photo.

"You do realize that Rochelle and I have been broken up
for quite a while now, don't you?" he asked.

A bitter taste soured his tongue at the mention of her
name. Memories of that day flashed through his mind like
a string of Polaroids. Their time together on the slopes, with
Rochelle wearing the hot-pink ski jacket he'd gifted her that
Christmas. The two of them cuddling in front of the main
lodge's fireplace while drinking spiked hot chocolate. Their
romantic seafood dinner at the Silver Lining restaurant, over-
looking the glaciers…

Dani threw her head back, her messy, sandy-brown pony-
tail swaying from side to side as she pointed toward the wall.
"Is this about the picture again?"

Troy glanced back up at it. His sister was standing on one side of him, her lean arms outstretched in a fun-loving pose. The siblings were smiling for the camera while Rochelle stood on the other side of Troy, gazing lovingly at him. He'd been so taken by her soft, elegant beauty and alluring demeanor.

Little had he known that she was a married woman. One minute he was thinking it was time to propose, and the next he was realizing their entire two-year relationship had been a complete lie.

"Yes," Troy responded. "This is about the picture again. I wish you'd take it down. Seeing it every time I'm in your office brings back memories I'd rather not relive over and over again."

"But I love that photo of us! Life was so good back then. Just fun and carefree." Dani paused when Troy's chin fell to his chest. "Fine. I'll *think* about taking it down. And if I do, I already have something to put in its spot." She opened a drawer and pulled out a bubble-wrapped package. "A certificate of appreciation from the community leaders."

"Well, thank you for at least considering my request. And congrats on the certificate."

"Thanks. Now, since we're on the subject of your dating life…"

"Were we, though?"

"In a roundabout way, yes, we were. I'm worried about you. You haven't dated anyone since you broke up with Rochelle."

"That is not true," Troy rebutted. "I've been out on plenty of dates since the breakup."

"Yeah, plenty of *first* dates. And then that's it. There haven't been any follow-ups, no second dates. You don't even give yourself an opportunity to get to know anybody!"

Troy's head rolled against the back of his chair. "Here we go again. Look, it's not my fault I haven't vibed with anyone since Rochelle. You act like I haven't tried. I did the whole matchmaking-through-friends thing. The dating-app thing. Hell, I even expanded my search beyond Arizona state lines! But there just wasn't a connection. And I'm not gonna force anything. So I'm just focusing on work, family, friends, community—"

"The gym," Dani interjected.

"Exactly. I've gotta stay in shape. Who else is gonna chase down all these criminals running around Maxwell?"

Tossing a coffee-stained napkin at him, she replied, "Listen, if you want to move back to Los Angeles and chase down crazed murderers all day, just say that. But you wouldn't be the man that you are today if not for your Maxwell upbringing. Giving back to your community is a privilege. So don't knock it. Plus, I need you here with me. There's nothing like having the support of a brother. Not to mention you're maintaining the Miller family's law enforcement legacy."

"You're right. Trust me, I'm grateful for this place. And proud of our family's legacy. It didn't take much convincing for me to move back. That right there should tell you how much my job means to me." Troy scooted away from the desk and stood. "Now, unless you've got something else for me, I need to get back to work and finish up those reports. I've got a pickup basketball game with the guys at Elliott Park that I don't want to be late for."

"All right, Officer Miller. Thanks again for checking on Mr. Diaz. Keep your head up. And I'm glad you're happy about staying in town."

Troy shuffled out of the office, wishing that what he'd just told his sister were true. He truly missed being involved in big cases and wondered if he'd made a mistake moving back home.

Chapter Two

"After an exhaustive ten-day search," Chloe said into the microphone, "authorities finally located Nadia Robinson's remains washed up along the shore of the Grand Calumet River. The river runs through Calumet City, a suburb about thirty minutes outside Chicago. Cell phone records led them to the body. Nadia's cause of death was asphyxiation, and DNA evidence found on her body matched that of her abusive ex-boyfriend, Randy Pierce."

Chloe's damp eyes burned as she glanced down at her podcast script. "An arrest warrant was issued, and authorities found Randy hiding out at his current girlfriend's apartment. He was charged with first-degree murder. The trial was delayed for months after Randy insisted on representing himself in court. Due to his lack of knowledge regarding the law and court procedures, the judge eventually appointed a public defender to him. In the end, the jury found Randy guilty. He was sentenced to life in prison without the possibility of parole."

After a brief pause, Chloe took a sip of wine, then ended with "Thank you again for tuning in to *Preyed Upon*. I'm your host, Cece Speaks, and I'll be back next week with another riveting true crime case. Until then, be kind, stay safe and remember to *always* trust your instincts."

She tapped the End Recording prompt on the laptop screen and removed her headphones. Refilling her glass with the last of the merlot, Chloe glanced at the length of the episode. One hour and twenty-three minutes. It was the longest of the three she'd recorded so far.

A cool breeze blew through her bedroom window, stirring the charcoal-gray blackout shades. A peek at the majestic White Mountains was a stark reminder that Chloe was back in Maxwell. While beautiful, the view was vastly different from the one she'd had back in Chicago, where her thirty-fourth-floor condo overlooked Lake Michigan and Navy Pier's colorfully lit Ferris wheel.

Even though she'd left the city almost two months ago, Chloe still missed it. The museums, diverse art scene, deep-dish pizza, Garrett's cheese-and-caramel popcorn…and of course her Chicago PD colleagues, who'd become more like family. But after the shoot-out at the Righteous Nation's headquarters, there was no way she could stay on the force. At least, that was what Superintendent Boyd thought.

"Sir, I can come back from this," Chloe had pleaded with him from her room inside Northwestern Memorial Hospital's Neurological Intensive Care Unit, where she was being treated for a concussion after the attack.

"Detective Grant, you almost got yourself killed. And after getting separated from the team, you put your entire unit in serious danger."

She'd jolted so abruptly that her monitor let off a two-tone alarm. "*I* put the unit in danger? How about the team left me alone in that basement to fend for myself!"

"Is that really how it went down? Or did the wires somehow get crossed? Were your directives as clear as they should've been? Either way, the ball got dropped. And let's not forget, that sting operation was formed under *your* leadership, Detective."

No amount of defending could sway the superintendent. But as he spoke, he could barely look Chloe in the eyes. Simply put, he knew that she'd been thorough, running through the plan with her colleagues dozens of times. Their failure to execute it properly was all in retaliation after she'd refused to lie to Internal Affairs on behalf of Justin.

"Listen," Superintendent Boyd continued, "the truth about the matter will eventually come out. But at this point, I think it would be in your best interest to step away from the Chicago PD. For your own safety as well as the department's."

The suggestion had stunned her into silence. Chloe knew she didn't have to take his advice. She could've argued her case and remained on the force. But her boss had been right about one thing—she no longer felt safe. Not after the way her team had left her hanging. So, after much contemplation and several tough conversations with her closest confidants, she'd decided to retire early and return to Maxwell.

Once Chloe began settling in back home, she realized all the Chicago trauma had followed her there. She'd spent many sleepless nights wondering whether she had done the right thing by standing in her truth. Or if she'd made any missteps that caused the sting operation to go left. What weighed the heaviest was whether she should've given in so easily and left the force.

One thing was for sure—racking her brain for answers hadn't aided in her healing. Neither had the self-inflicted torment triggered by her retirement. Chloe had desperately needed an outlet to take her mind off of things. *Dateline*'s 24/7 streaming channel worked for a while, but she longed for something deeper.

Luckily, she'd found that after accidentally stumbling

upon a true crime podcast playlist on Spotify. Deep dives into criminal behavior and justice for the victims reignited the fire that had sparked Chloe's desire to work in law enforcement. So much so that she'd decided to launch a podcast of her own, focusing on women who'd been stalked, harassed and murdered.

Three weeks after returning to Maxwell, Chloe recorded her first episode of *Preyed Upon*. For safety reasons, she'd chosen to go by the pseudonym Cece Speaks. She hadn't told many people where she was going before leaving Chicago. Keeping her true identity under wraps meant her enemies couldn't retaliate, nor could they trace the podcast back to her.

The first case Chloe covered was about Farrah Thornton, a college student from North Carolina who'd been at odds with her jealous roommate. Things between the friends-turned-enemies came to a head when the roommate's boyfriend became obsessed with Farrah.

One evening, the roommate returned to their off-campus apartment to find Farrah brutally murdered. After an extensive investigation, DNA evidence linked both the roommate and her boyfriend to the vicious attack.

Chloe had been so eager to check the analytics after the episode went live. The number of listeners was decent. But *Preyed Upon* hadn't reached the overnight-sensation status she'd seen other podcasters achieve. So she sharpened her editing skills, delved a little deeper when researching the cases and created social media accounts before recording episode two.

The second case was about Peyton Carter, a young woman from Michigan who'd been living a double life, unbeknownst to her overprotective parents. One of her secret boyfriends found out about the other and, in a jealous rage, stabbed her to death on her front porch.

Bzzz...

Chloe's head whipped in the direction of her vibrating cell phone. A reminder of Maxwell's opening day at the fall farmers market popped up. Behind it was the phone's lock-screen wallpaper—a photo of her celebrating last year's Christmas party with the Chicago PD.

The sight pulled at something in Chloe's chest. Her bright smile, as she stood arm in arm with Justin, represented how she'd felt during the majority of her time with the department. There was a period when her colleagues brought her nothing but pure joy. Their bond was impenetrable. Or so she'd thought. Nevertheless, the picture was an ultimate throwback to the good times. The times she'd give anything to go back to...

You need to delete that.

Grabbing her purse, Chloe shook off the sentiments and headed toward the door of her rented three-bedroom town house. Sitting around mulling over the past wasn't doing her any good. So maybe figuring out whether to buy avocados for guacamole or tomatoes for salsa would.

"Hey, girl! When did you get to town?"

Chloe almost dropped the chili peppers in her hand at the screechy voice approaching from behind. Spinning around, she let off a resounding whoop at the sight of her former high school friend and debate team captain, Jasmine Bailey.

"It's too early for you to be home for the holidays, isn't it?" Jasmine's voice was muffled by the shoulder of Chloe's cropped denim jacket as she embraced her tightly. "It's only October. Plus, I know the temperatures in Chicago aren't freezing just yet, which means..."

"Which means crime rates are still high and the city needs as many officers on the streets as possible. I know."

Chloe took a step back, contemplating just how much she should divulge. Since returning to Maxwell, that had been an ongoing dilemma. Only those closest to her knew that she'd retired from the force early and why. Now that she was getting out more and running into old acquaintances, she needed to come up with a reason behind her return.

"I love your goddess locs," Chloe said, hoping to buy herself some time. "Where did you get them done?"

"Loctastic. It's a salon located in Scottsdale. I can put you in touch with my hairdresser, if you'd like. It isn't easy getting an appointment, though. So if you want your hair done, you may not be able to get in for a couple of months."

"Thanks. I'll keep that in mind in case I decide to switch up my look."

"Well, the long, flowing bob is certainly working for you," Jasmine said, flipping Chloe's hair over her shoulder. "You look great. Chicago always has agreed with you. Speaking of which, how are things going out in the Midwest? Last time we talked, you'd just been promoted to detective, and you were consulting on that television show. What's the name of it again?"

"The Chicago Force."

"Yes! I loved the first few episodes. Ooh! And you were dating that *fine* attorney who'd just made partner, Adam Hamilton—"

"You mean Alex Harrison," Chloe interjected, fanning her face with the farmers-market directory. "Yeah…a lot's changed since the last time we spoke."

"Well, we should get together and catch up. How long are you gonna be in town?"

"Am I imagining things?" a deep, throaty voice crooned

from the other side of the vegetable stand. "Or is that Chloe Grant I see standing before me?"

The women's heads swiveled in unison. Chloe's chin slowly dipped at the sight of a tall, broad-shouldered, ridiculously handsome man who looked somewhat familiar.

"Hmm," Jasmine sighed. "Where have I seen that guy?"

"I'm not sure. But he seems to know who I am."

"Lucky you. Oop, and he's coming this way. That's my cue to exit stage left. Let's talk soon!"

As Jasmine hurried off, Chloe quickly ran her hands through her hair, her lips pulling into an apprehensive smile. "Hi. I'm sorry, but, um, do we…?" She hesitated, embarrassed to admit that she had no idea who he was.

"Know one another? We do. But we haven't actually *seen* each other in years. So I wouldn't expect for you to remember me at first glance."

The more he spoke, the more that voice teased at her memory. And his mannerisms—the sexy half grin that drew her gaze to his lush, kissable lips. The three tiny crinkles around his shining, deep brown eyes. Those robust hands pushing up the sleeves on his black track jacket, exposing his muscular forearms.

"But judging by your expression," he continued, "I'm guessing my identity is starting to ring a bell. Or at least that's what I hope is putting a smile on your face."

"Troy Miller," Chloe said with a snap of her finger. "You know, despite being a whole five years younger than me, you always have been a little charmer."

"As if five years is a huge gap. But it's nice to know you still find me charming. And in case you hadn't noticed, these days, there is nothing *little* about me."

You've got that right, Chloe almost blurted, fanning her face with the directory once again.

"Hey, was that Jasmine Bailey you were just talking to?" he asked.

"It was. You remember her, too?"

"I do. But clearly she doesn't remember me, the way she ran off without even saying hello. I'm used to it, though. I know I look different than I did back when I was still living here in Maxwell. A little taller, a little bulkier..."

A little was an understatement. Chloe, however, kept the comment to herself. No need to ignite the embers of attraction smoldering inside her chest.

The sensation was inexplicable considering she and Troy practically grew up together. Chloe and his sister, Dani, were once the best of friends. When Troy moved away for college, Dani would give her regular updates on his LA activities. But then the two friends fell out, and Chloe didn't feel comfortable contacting Troy behind his sister's back. So she lost touch with the Miller family altogether.

"So what are you doing back in Maxwell?" Troy asked. "It's a little early for you to be here for the holidays, isn't it?"

Here we go again... Chloe thought. Only this time she didn't feel the need to evade the truth. Behind the glint of sexiness in Troy's piercing gaze was a warmth that somehow disarmed her, making her feel safe enough to open up.

Staring down at her brown suede riding boots, she kicked at a crack in the dusty gray asphalt. "I, um... It's a long story, actually."

He nodded toward his Apple Watch, barely glancing at the screen. "I've got time. That is, if you do."

"I do."

"Okay, then. I'll tell you what. Why don't you let me treat you to one of Hazel's peanut-butter-and-banana smoothies? We can grab a table and catch up on everything we've missed. It's been a lot, hasn't it?"

"It really has."

That glint in Troy's eyes disappeared, replaced by a dimness pouring through his lowered lids. Chloe sensed what hadn't been said—a lot had happened since she and his sister stopped speaking.

"I'd love a smoothie," she told him, despite the bout of queasiness now churning through her gut. Chloe hadn't thought about her and Dani's broken friendship in a long while, let alone the devastating way it had ended.

"So you'd love a smoothie," he said with a smirk, "but no sit-down, no catch-up, *nothing*?"

"Oh, no!" Chloe insisted, reaching out and running her hand along his shoulder blade.

As Troy's face lit up with amusement, Chloe jerked her hand away.

"Sorry," she continued. "But I didn't mean it like that. I'd love to sit down and catch up, too."

"You sure?"

"I'm positive. Lead the way."

Pull yourself together, Chloe's inner voice advised as she followed him to Hazel's stand.

On the way there, she could barely focus on his small talk, as his side profile appeared eerily similar to Dani's. The slight hump in the bridge of his nose. The way his nostrils flared when he laughed. The angled jawline and tiny cleft in his chin.

The likeness sent a pang of remorse straight through Chloe. Her vision clouded as reels of their friendship rolled through her mind. All the firsts they'd experienced together. The first day of school, from kindergarten through senior year of college. The first time they conquered Cole's Ski Resort's Max Mountain. Their first dates and first heartbreaks.

But the biggest first they'd planned to share was joining

Maxwell PD's training academy and becoming police officers. That had been their agenda since childhood, back when Dani and Troy's father took over as chief of police.

Shortly after college graduation, however, everything changed. Chloe took a trip to Chicago and met Alex, an up-and-coming attorney who'd just hit the 40 Under 40 list in *Crain's Chicago Business*. He was a hotshot. A handsome, polished man about town who'd left Chloe smitten after introducing himself at her hotel's swanky rooftop bar.

His slate-gray eyes dazzled against his smooth, tawny skin when he laughed at her jokes. His charismatic swagger mixed with several cocktails led to a passionate evening that morphed into a weeklong fling. Chloe thought it would end there. But when the big-city bachelor asked her to come back and visit him later that month, she couldn't say no.

Ten years her senior, Alex was everything Chloe strove to be. His work ethic was unmatched. The dedication to his clients was unwavering. And his commitment to healthy living was steadfast. That, on top of the fact that their lovemaking was the best she'd ever experienced, had her moving to Chicago within their first year of dating.

Their relationship was like a fairy tale. A whirlwind she was sure would lead to marriage. While awaiting his proposal, Chloe had fulfilled her lifelong dream of becoming a police officer, making everything seem perfect. But while focusing on becoming Mrs. Harrison, she'd lost her best friend in the process.

"*Hello*, earth to Chloe."

Her head swiveled in Troy's direction. She'd sunk so deep into the depths of her past that she hadn't realized they'd reached the smoothie stand.

"Are you all right?" he asked.

"Yes. I—I'm fine. Sorry, what were you saying?"

"I was asking whether you want a small or a large."

"Oh, a small is fine. Thanks."

He moved ahead in line without taking his eyes off her. "Where did your mind wander off to just now?"

A shrug of her shoulders was all the response she could muster.

Nodding slowly, he gave her a wink. "Got it. You don't want to talk about it. Okay. I'll leave it alone. For now, at least."

Once their order was filled, the pair remained relatively quiet while squeezing through the crowd toward the last available picnic table. The seating area had been set up near a unicorn bouncy house, where children's laughter whizzed through the air. Families, couples and groups of friends filled every inch of the vicinity. All of Maxwell's residents appeared to be in attendance. For Chloe, she was glad to have run into just one of them—Troy.

Taking a seat across from him, she picked the conversation back up. "So when was the last time you and I ran into one another?"

"It's been years, hasn't it? I did keep up with you on social media from time to time. And through Dani, of course. At least until…you know."

"Yeah, same. I do love how we both got out of Maxwell and experienced life in a big city. How did you like living in Los Angeles?"

"It was cool. I loved swimming for USC and met some great people. But being a paramedic in the City of Angels was wild. I saw it all. Stabbings, shootings and overdoses were a daily occurrence. I'm sure you can relate, being that you're a detective in Chicago. Which, by the way, I hope you'll be here long enough for us to hang out at some point. When are you heading back?"

"Yeah, about that…"

Troy side-eyed her curiously while sipping his smoothie. *Just tell him.*

"I'm actually in town for good. I took an early retirement. It's, um, it's a long story. But yeah. I'm back in Maxwell permanently."

"Oh, really? Okay, well, judging by the way you're making eye contact with everyone but me, is it safe to assume you don't wanna talk about it?"

Chloe shoved her fidgety hands underneath the table and stared straight at him. "I'd rather not get into all the salacious details. At least, not right now. But long story short, I was working with the police department's tactical gang unit, and we were on the cusp of taking down one of the city's most notorious organizations."

"Which one?"

"The Righteous Nation."

"Mmm-hmm," Troy grunted, his fist tapping the table's peeling white surface. "I've heard of them. They're affiliated with a crew in LA. When word got out that there was a decline in Chicago's gang leadership, the West Coast affiliates tried to help the Righteous Nation take over their rival's territory."

"Let me guess whose exact territory. The Reckless Assassins?"

"Yep. That's them."

"Ironically, that gang played an indirect part in my retirement. But anyway, my unit was working to take down the leaders of the Righteous Nation when a sting operation went bad. *Really* bad. My team left me alone inside the Nation's headquarters, and I was confronted by four heavily armed members. Just as I was about to be kidnapped, the unit finally showed up. Afterward, the superintendent suggested I step away from the force. No one had my back. And the higher-ups refused to take an honest look at the corruption within the department. So for the sake of my own safety and everyone else's, I left. Now here I am. Of course, there's more to it than that. But we can talk about it another day."

"Of course. You don't have to get too deep into it. But wait—does that mean you're planning on talking to me again after today?"

The question was followed by a chuckle that put his gleaming white teeth on full display.

Chloe swayed in her seat, murmuring, "I'd certainly like to. If you would…"

"Oh, I absolutely would. Now, on a different note, since you're back in Maxwell for good, does that mean you'll be joining our police force?"

Her cup almost fell from her hand. "You're joking, right?"

"No. I'm dead serious. You'd be a great addition to the department."

"Is your sister still the chief of police?"

"She is."

"Then the answer is no."

Troy tossed his hands in the air, his face wrinkled in disdain. "Aww, come on, Chloe! You and Dani used to be the best of friends."

"Keys words—*used* to be. Trust me, I'm the last person Dani wants to see, let alone work with."

"So I'm assuming you haven't reached out to her since you moved back?"

"I have not. And why would I? Like I said, she doesn't wanna hear from me."

"You don't know that for a fact," he argued, his tone softening as he twirled his cup between his fingers. "And you won't know until you try."

"Troy, Dani and I haven't spoken in years. I don't think there's any hope for a reconciliation."

"Wait—remind me why you two fell out in the first place."

Chloe hesitated, searching his face for a hint that he already knew the answer but wanted to hear her side of things. But the deep creases lining his forehead confirmed a genuine curiosity.

"You two never talked about it?" she asked.

"No. I've tried, but whenever I'd bring up your name, she would just say you all grew apart, then change the subject. To be honest, her response always seemed rooted in hurt rather than anger. So, what happened?"

The weight of the question fell heavily between them. She leaned into the table, her skin stinging with embarrassment. She hated to admit that it all boiled down to her relationship with Alex.

"Well, the reason I moved to Chicago was because I fell in love with this guy, Alex—"

"Lucky bastard," Troy interrupted, punctuating the statement with a wink.

When she tossed him a head-tilting look of *I'm being serious*, he threw in, "Just trying to lighten the mood. Go on. I'm listening."

Chloe couldn't deny the fact that his lighthearted charm was downright endearing. Being in his presence felt good, which made sense considering he was a part of her most precious memories. All the days she'd spent hanging out at his family's home inside their huge basement, playing Uno and listening to hip-hop music while eating Cheetos and pepperoni pizza bites. She and Dani would always try to get rid of Troy. But once he kicked off spontaneous comedy routines or shared gossip about their friends that they hadn't heard, they'd let him stick around.

"You're doing it again," Troy said, reaching across the table and nudging her hand.

"Doing what again?"

"Drifting into space while we're in the middle of a conversation. Where did that mind of yours go this time?"

"I was thinking about you, actually. And Dani. And how much fun we used to have back in the day."

"Oh, yeah. We did have some great times. Hopefully there will be more of that since we're both back home. I'm convinced that whatever you and Dani fell out over can be resolved."

He paused, as if awaiting a response. Chloe didn't give him one.

Clearing his throat, he said, "But anyway, back to your story. Tell me how this Alex guy broke up the friendship."

"Well, it all boils down to Dani knowing what was best for me when I couldn't see it for myself."

"What do you mean?"

"Turns out Alex wasn't the good guy he'd presented himself to be. I knew he had a reputation for being somewhat of a player. But when I came along, he swore those days were behind him and he was ready to settle down. He proved that to be true. At least, for a while he did. There was a time when we'd even discussed getting married. Then a high-profile murder case landed on his desk, and all talk of our future stopped. That case consumed him. Late nights turned into all-nighters away from the house…"

"Humph. Yeah, I can definitely relate to that."

"You can? How so?"

Troy's eyes darted wildly as he pulled at his goatee. "I— I'm sorry. I didn't mean to interrupt you. Go on."

"No, you didn't interrupt me. I wanna hear what you have to say. You can relate to what I'm telling you?"

"I can."

"In what way?" Chloe pressed.

Pulling at his collar, Troy blew an exasperated sigh. "You know what? I'm really enjoying myself right now, and I'd hate to dampen the mood. So can we table that discussion for another day?"

"Of course we can. So wait—does that mean you're planning on talking to me again after today?" Chloe added jokingly.

"Oh, so you're mocking me now?" he shot back with a charismatic laugh. "Nah, but seriously. I'm not doing the whole fake *we've gotta stay in touch* thing. When I say it, I mean it. We should connect again."

"We definitely should," she murmured, the pull of attraction swirling within her long pause. "So, um, anyway. Like I was saying, I thought Alex was spending all that time away from home because he was working on the case. I'm aware that attorneys put in ridiculously long hours while doing massive amounts of research. But I eventually found out it wasn't just business that was keeping him away."

"Oh, no. Don't tell me."

"Yeah. He was having an affair with a woman named Melissa Chaney. You may have heard of her. She's a pretty well-known paralegal who also works as a social media influencer. Her OnlyFans account has over fifty thousand followers."

"Oh, wow. And her firm doesn't have a problem with that?"

"I think she knows where to draw the line so that there won't be too much controversy. But from what I've heard, her account is pretty racy."

Troy nodded, stirring his straw inside the cup while watching Chloe intently. "I'm sorry you went through that. One thing I do remember is how Dani never thought that guy was good enough for you."

"And she was right. But it wasn't just my relationship with Alex that affected our friendship. Dani was hurt when I decided to join the Chicago PD. She felt like I was being disloyal to Maxwell, especially after we'd made a pact to become police officers together back when we were kids. But things change when you think you've found the love of your life, you know?"

"Yes. I do know."

Troy's voice grew faint as he stared off into the distance.

"Now you're doing it," she told him.

"Doing what?"

"Getting in your head. Watch how quickly I turn the tables by asking what's going on inside *your* mind."

A throaty laugh oozed from his lips. "Aww, okay. Let's just say that when it comes to relationships, you are not alone in having to bounce back from disappointment. And as tough of a guy as I am, I'm not afraid to admit that my last relationship left me pretty brokenhearted. But again, we're tabling all that for another day. For now…" He paused, checking the time on his cell. "I should probably get back to the station. I told Dani I was just gonna stop by here and grab a smoothie. I'm sure she's wondering where I am."

"Wait—you're working for Maxwell PD now?"

"I am. Once my dad retired and Dani was promoted to chief, I decided to come home and join the force. I sensed that she could use the support. You know how Dani is. Too prideful to come right out and tell you how she feels sometimes."

"*Sometimes*. But not all the time. She had no qualms expressing how she felt when I told her I was moving to Chicago. That woman insisted I was abandoning her, abandoning our hometown, breaking our bond…all for a man who hadn't earned my love. But anyway, it's awesome that you're working for the department. And I'm sure Dani appreciates it."

"She does. But this place is way different from LA. I had to get used to the slower pace. Here I'm dealing with moving violations, disorderly conduct and kids stealing sodas from gas stations. Or noise complaints from residents whose neighbors are playing their music too loud."

"What about the drag-racing teenagers? Are they still a problem?"

"Oh, they're worse than ever. That's a tradition that's never gonna end. But other than those types of petty crimes, there isn't much happening around here."

"Well, considering we just came from two of the biggest cities in the country, we could probably both use the break."

"I guess so," Troy agreed as the pair made their way toward the parking lot. "Listen, I'd love to get together again soon, if that's okay with you?"

"Yeah, I'd like that. I really enjoyed this little impromptu get-together. Plus, we still have a lot to catch up on. I didn't tell you about the true crime podcast I've launched." When Troy's mouth fell open with surprise, Chloe pressed her finger against his lips. "But *shh*. No one knows that it's me behind the mic. After the way things went down back in Chicago, I'm keeping a low profile. I didn't even tell most of the people there that I was moving back to Maxwell."

"Your secret is safe with me. And I'm a huge true crime fan, so I can't wait to hear all about it. Speaking of which…" Troy handed her his cell. "Save your number in my phone and I'll shoot you a text so that you'll have mine."

"Good idea," Chloe said, struggling to enter her contact info correctly under his intense gaze.

"I cannot wait to tell Dani that I ran into you. Once she

finds out you're back in town, I'm sure the past will be forgotten and she'll want to see you."

"I don't know about all that. But it would be nice to get together. It's been way too long."

When Chloe stopped at her car, Troy opened the door and leaned in. "It's been way too long for us, too. I'll reach out soon to set something up."

"Looking forward to it."

Right before she climbed inside, he put his hand on her arm. Her calf muscles stiffened as she braced herself for what appeared to be an incoming kiss. But instead of puckering up, his lips pulled an unhurried smile.

"Um, Troy, you'd better go…"

The soft-spoken words rasped against the back of her throat. She stood there, waiting for him to leave so she could watch him walk away. But he didn't, instead remaining planted right next to her.

The buzz of his cell phone pulled them apart.

"That's Dani. Probably calling to find out where I am." He shoved the phone inside his pocket, then slowly backed away. "It was so good seeing you. We'll be talking soon."

"Sounds good."

Chloe hadn't known what to expect upon her return to Maxwell. But the one thing she never would've bet on was standing in the middle of a parking lot, reconnecting with Troy Miller.

Chapter Three

"This is just really strange," Jasmine whimpered while vigorously rubbing her hands over her arms. "And creepy as hell."

"I know it is," Troy said. "But trust that we're gonna do everything we can to get to the bottom of it."

It was late Saturday morning. His day off. He'd been anticipating the afternoon all week long as he and Chloe made plans to hang out at Cole's Ski Resort. Right before he'd jumped in the shower, Dani texted him saying that Jasmine Bailey had called 9-1-1 to report a suspicious package that had been left at her front door. Since he'd taken a hazardous-materials training course, Dani asked that he go check it out.

How ironic, Troy texted back. I hadn't seen Jasmine since I've been back in Maxwell and recently caught a glimpse of her earlier this week at the farmers market.

By the time he'd arrived on the scene, officers had already begun collecting evidence and interviewing Jasmine. Troy quickly pulled on a protective suit, full-face breathing apparatus and chemical-resistant gloves, then got to work.

After moving the package a safe distance away from the house, he carefully untied its cream satin bow and peeled open the beige kraft paper. Inside was a bundle of dead flower stems. The petals had been removed. And the thorns had been painted a bright shade of red.

"What the hell...?"

Troy sifted through each stem, careful not to disrupt the withered, blackened stalks and sharp-edged leaflets. There were no signs of hazardous powders or liquids.

"See anything that looks suspicious?" Officer Keller had shouted from the front porch.

"No, not yet!"

He'd snapped a few photos of the stems, placed them inside an evidence bag and stored it in the trunk before rejoining the team. Several officers were combing the white stucco Spanish Colonial's entryway, dusting the natural stone porch for finger- and shoe prints. Tossing Officer Keller a head nod, he directed him toward a quiet corner inside the courtyard and opened his phone's camera roll.

"This is what was inside of that package. Dead flower stems with the petals cut off. I didn't see any immediate sign of poisoning, but we'll know more once tests are run at the forensics lab. But wait—check out the thorns." Troy paused, enlarging the photo. "Some sick bastard took the time to paint them red."

"To represent what? Blood?"

"That's what I'm thinking."

"*Humph.* I bet one of her exes is behind this."

When Troy noticed Jasmine watching them, he muttered, "You and I are on the same page."

Officer Keller reached inside a brown paper evidence bag and handed him a small white envelope. "Here, check this out. Discreetly."

Troy took a look around before peeling it open. It took a few tries before he was able to yank the thick card-stock paper from inside.

Neatly handwritten in small black lettering was a message:

You didn't see me. But I loved seeing you. From a distance, of course. I promise the next time will be up close and personal. PS—Those black Nike trainers look awesome on you...

His hand stiffened as he slid the card back inside the envelope. The threat prompted him to search the perimeter of the house for surveillance cameras. A quick scan of the red tile roof and arched front doorway revealed none.

"Do you know if Jasmine has any sort of security system installed?"

"She doesn't. A couple of officers spoke to neighbors in the vicinity who have surveillance equipment. Unfortunately, their cameras don't capture footage around Jasmine's house. But hold on a second. Back to that note. I asked Jasmine about the Nike trainers this person mentioned. She owns a pair. And she's only worn them one time."

"When was that?" Troy asked.

"Earlier this week, at the farmers market."

"Interesting," he muttered while frantically typing notes into his phone's app. "I was just talking about how crime in this town usually consists of moving violations and disorderly conduct. Who would've thought I'd be investigating some weirdo leaving dead flower stems with fake bloody thorns on an old high school acquaintance's doorstep?"

"I know, right? I'm just hoping this doesn't escalate any further," Officer Keller said right before Troy's phone buzzed.

"Hold on. This is Chief Miller texting me."

Just got an update from Officer Thomas. Thanks for getting to the scene so quickly. Hope I didn't ruin your snowboarding outing with the guys...

Guilt throbbed inside Troy's head as he typed, You didn't ruin anything. I told them I had some business to take care of and would catch up with them later.

Sounds good. Go on and enjoy yourself. I'll have the team finish up at the scene.

On the way to his car, Troy sent Chloe a text asking if she was still up for hanging out.

Please say yes…

Another wave of remorse hit the moment he pressed Send. Troy hated that he'd lied to his sister. But he couldn't bring himself to tell her that he was meeting up with Chloe. Not after the way she'd reacted when he told her Chloe had moved back to Maxwell.

"She *what*?" Dani had screeched. Before he could repeat himself, she'd continued with "Well, I hope you didn't suggest she reach out to me. Or that we should all get together. I haven't spoken to that woman in years. And after the way she dropped everybody and everything for that Chi-town slickster, I don't plan on starting now."

"First of all, *ouch*," Troy had replied. "Second of all, whatever went down between you and Chloe is none of my business. So I'm staying out of it. Third of all, come on, sis. All that happened years ago. You and Chloe were the best of friends. Imagine how she feels now after that relationship didn't work out. I'm sure she's filled with regret. And I know she hates the way your friendship ended. Maybe if you all just sat down and talked—"

"I'm sorry," Dani had interrupted, glaring at him through

squinted eyes. "But I could've sworn you said you were staying out of it."

That was all it took to shut Troy up. Since that conversation, he hadn't mentioned Chloe's name again.

He approached his black Ford Mustang Mach-E and popped the trunk. As he tossed his protective gear inside a biohazard waste bag, his cell buzzed. The sight of Chloe's name flashing across the screen was like a soothing balm, releasing the tension swirling through his chest.

My day is open, her message read. I'd love to hang out if you're still up for it. Let me know and I'll meet you at Cole's.

Troy's fingers were a blur as they flew across the screen confirming he was on his way there. By the time he drove off, his feelings of guilt had been surpassed by an urgency to see Chloe again.

"No worries. Thanks again," Troy told the attendant at the resort's reservation desk before he joined Chloe by the grand fireplace.

"Any luck?" she asked.

"No, unfortunately. There aren't any snowboarding reservations left. And it looks like the slopes are packed with skiers. So we've only got a few options. There's snow tubing and sledding, which both have wait lists, or a horse-drawn sleigh ride around the premises. Warm blankets and hot chocolate included."

"Hmm," Chloe sighed, tapping her fingertips against the activity booklet.

As she contemplated their options, Troy took a seat next to her on the russet leather love seat, struggling not to stare. Chloe had never been one to rest on the laurels of her beauty. But there was no denying that she'd always been the prettiest girl in their neighborhood with her soft brown eyes, free-flowing curls and lithe, curvy figure maintained by their community's running club.

"I think I'm in the mood for a sleigh ride," she decided, her puckered lips accentuated by a shimmer of pink gloss. "That way we can really talk and catch up."

"Okay, then. A sleigh ride it is. The next one leaves in fifteen minutes. I already put our names on the list just in case."

Chloe hopped up, pressing her hands together as they headed toward the exit. "A man who knows how to take the initiative. I like that."

"Do you now? I'll have to keep that in mind."

Troy clenched his jaw, hoping he hadn't gone too far. Judging by her smirk, he hadn't.

He placed his hand on the small of Chloe's back and led her out the door. Cole's had been the perfect choice for their first outing. Its familiarity granted an immediate air of comfort. As they were growing up, their families had spent countless days inside the lofty, timber-framed lodge, lounging on the European-style furnishings while sipping hot apple cider. Natural light poured in through the expansive glass windows, offering breathtaking views of the snowcapped peaks and deep valleys below.

"Ooh, it's chilly out here," Chloe said, staring up at the stream of flurries swirling through the breeze.

She clutched Troy's arm while they hurried toward the cedar pergola waiting area. Infrared lamps hung from the gabled roof, offering up cozy waves of heat. Despite the warmth floating through the area, Chloe's body remained pressed against his.

He capitalized on the move, wrapping an arm around her. "So, tell me more about what life was like when you moved away. What did you do for fun back in Chicago?"

"Well, here's a cool fact. Did you know that I did some consulting work on the television show *The Chicago Force*?"

"No. I didn't. I love that show. What type of consulting were you doing?"

"I was a technical adviser. Since the show's style is a ripped-from-the-headlines-type theme, producers wanted the storylines to be as authentic as possible. So I was there to ensure that the scenes followed accurate policies and procedures."

"Wow. That's awesome, Chloe. You know, now that I think about it, those plots did emulate real-life crime stories. Like the one where the girl's mother had Munchausen syndrome by proxy and forced her daughter to get all those unnecessary medical treatments."

"Yes. And the daughter and her boyfriend ended up killing her. That episode won *The Chicago Force* an Emmy."

"Were the actors good people off the set? I'm a huge fan of the guy who plays the rookie cop, Max Feldman."

"Oh, yeah. The actors are really cool. And Max is one of the nicest people on the show. I loved working with the entire cast and crew. Well, except for the head writer. I couldn't stand him. He always gave me the hardest time…"

Chloe's voice trailed off as hooves clopped along the pewter paver stones. Two massive chestnut draft horses stopped in front of the pergola with a burgundy sleigh in tow.

Slipping his hand in hers, Troy helped Chloe climb on board. They slid into the last row of seats, cozying up underneath a cream blanket while waiting for the other passengers to settle in.

"So, back to our convo," Troy said. "Who is this head writer and why was he giving you a hard time?"

"His name is Simon Grazer. And he didn't like how I'd

call him out on his inaccurate portrayals. To say he wasn't interested in authenticity and fact-checking would be an understatement. As long as the dialogue was hard-hitting and the shots looked good, he was happy. He didn't care whether the writing aligned with Chicago's guidelines. Whenever I'd step in and correct him, he'd accuse me of being a disruption and demand that I be fired. But the producers weren't having it. They usually sided with me."

"No surprise there. I'm sure you were on top of your game. And I'm not surprised to hear about Simon's negligence, either. I met several people who work in the entertainment industry during my time in LA. It didn't take long to see how much of that business is smoke and mirrors. Nothing is what it seems, and the number one goal is to get ahead by any means necessary."

"Exactly. But it took me a minute to realize that." Chloe hesitated, staring past Troy and out at the snow-dusted pine-tree clusters. "When I first landed that job, I thought it was so exciting. So glamorous…getting to know the actors, watching production build those elaborate sets, seeing the scenes I'd worked on actually come to life. It was great. For the most part. But the disagreements with Simon really ruined the good vibes. We once got into it over whether or not the state of Illinois has a stand-your-ground statute. Simon insisted that it does. But it doesn't. And I told him that, explaining how citizens *are* allowed to defend themselves to prevent a forcible felony, yet there is no actual law in place. Simon, however, kept telling me I was wrong. He jumped in my face and started yelling and swinging his arms everywhere. I actually thought he might hit me."

"*Hit* you? Wow. It got that intense?" Troy asked right before the sleigh took off.

"It did, unfortunately…"

Silence fell over the pair. He glanced down at Chloe's delicate, freshly manicured hand, her slender fingers spread across her thigh. It took everything in him not to reach over and wrap them in his grip.

"So how did the argument end?" Troy asked. "Did you put this guy in a headlock and threaten to arrest him?"

"Ha! I should have. But, luckily, I didn't have to. Brody Rogers, who was the head of security, stepped in and straightened him out. After that, Simon was suspended from the set for a few episodes and never tried me again. Nobody did, actually."

"Well, I'm glad to hear somebody came forward and intervened." Troy noticed her staring down at her lap instead of the scenic landscape. Taking it as a cue to drop the subject, he leaned against the back of the seat and propped his arm behind her.

The pair grew silent once again as they took in the sparkling blankets of snow covering the terrain. Rows of mixed fir and aspen trees stood majestically in the distance as skiers flew down the slopes. While cruising the piste together would've been cool, Troy was perfectly content with their intimate tour of the resort.

"So, this podcast of yours," he said. "What's the name of it?"

Chloe's lips curled into a soft smile as her shoulders relaxed against Troy's forearm. *"Preyed Upon."*

"Ooh, I like that. Sounds very suspenseful. I'm definitely gonna have to check it out."

"I'd really appreciate that. This endeavor really means a lot to me. I was so upset, the way everything went down when I left the Chicago PD. Then when I returned to Maxwell, I was just…so *lost*. It felt like I no longer had a place or a purpose in life. I needed something that would occupy my mind and fuel my hunger to tackle criminal justice. This podcast has been the perfect remedy."

Troy pulled out his cell phone and opened Spotify. When he typed the podcast's name into the search bar, a black-and-white photo of a dense, foggy wooded area appeared on the screen.

"Is this you?"

"Yep, that's me."

"But wait—who is Cece Speaks?"

"Oh, that's the name that I go by. I didn't wanna use my real name. Between my ex, his new girlfriend, Simon, several police officers back in Chicago… I just don't want certain people knowing what I'm doing."

"Understood. And as for your ex, I still can't believe he cheated on you. What a fool. Did he ever try and win you back after the breakup?"

"He did. In his narcissistic mind, he just knew a little charm and a few gifts would do the trick. But I was completely done. Then once Alex realized it was over for good, all hell broke loose."

"See, I can already tell we're about to venture into unpleasant territory," Troy muttered, a slight chuckle bubbling underneath the statement. "Because you're about to get started, then I'm probably gonna get started…"

"I know, right? It's as if nothing good has happened to us since we left Maxwell! But hey, it is what it is. You and I both seem to have moved on. Had it been left up to Alex, though, he'd still be trying to convince me that the situation with his new girlfriend was just a fling. *A mistake*, he called it."

"Man, this conversation is so triggering."

"I'm sorry, Troy. Let's just change the subject."

"No. Please. It's not triggering in a bad way. It just reminds me of my ex. We dated for two years and I was actually thinking about proposing."

"Why didn't you?"

"Because she was already married."

Chloe's body shifted so abruptly that she almost fell out of the sleigh. "Excuse me, but she was *what*?"

"Already. *Married*." The words singed his tongue as they escaped his lips. Troy resisted the urge to gather a scoop of snow and cool his palate. "Anyway, don't get me started. I'm starting to sound like the president of the wounded-hearts club. Go on. Finish your story. It's way more interesting than mine."

"You sure? Because I'm here to listen, if you want to share."

"I'm positive."

"Okay, well, Alex's new girlfriend, Melissa, eventually found out that he'd been reaching out, trying to get me back. Let's just say that didn't sit well with her. She started calling me incessantly, demanding that I back off, as if *I* was the one pursuing *him*. The woman even threatened me a few times. I should've arrested her for harassment." Chloe hesitated, staring out at a couple of elk feeding in the distance. "You know, maybe it was a good thing that I got the hell out of Chicago."

"I think it was. But I'm probably being biased, since my opinion is solely based on the fact that we've reconnected."

Turning to him, Chloe murmured, "I couldn't agree more."

Troy held her gaze, shifting against the bench when her soft palm caressed the top of his hand. "So, back to this podcast of yours. What types of cases are you covering?"

"Mostly women who've experienced some sort of domestic violence. The episode I published last week was so creepy. It was about a woman who'd been stalked and harassed by her ex-husband. He ended up killing her."

"That's so tragic. What was it about this case that made it so creepy?"

"Well, a week before she was found stabbed to death on her front porch, someone delivered a strange package to her front door. She didn't think it'd been left by her ex because she had just secured a restraining order against him. So the woman opened the package, and inside of it was a bundle of dead flower stems."

Troy's head fell to one side. "Wait—what was inside the package?"

"Dead flower stems," Chloe repeated, her shoulders shivering as she spoke. "But get this. The petals had been cut off, and the thorns were painted red. *Ew.* Can you imagine?"

"Yes, actually. I one hundred percent can."

"What do you mean?"

"You're not gonna believe this, but I was called out to Jasmine Bailey's house this morning because somebody had left a weird-looking parcel on her doorstep. When I opened it, there were dead flower stems inside with thorns that had been painted red."

Chloe's mouth hollowed as her entire face froze. Her hand slid onto Troy's forearm, tightening on his coat sleeve. "Please tell me you're joking."

"No, I'm totally serious. Do you think that was just a coincidence? Or did someone steal that idea after listening to your podcast?"

He awaited her response. But Chloe just sat there, clutching her face while shaking her head from side to side.

"What is the likelihood that someone you just so happen to know," Troy continued, "would experience something that obscure, right around the time you aired that episode?"

"It's got to be a coincidence. Because so few people even

know that I'm the person behind the mic. Did Jasmine mention who she thinks may have done it?"

"No, not as far as I know. Whoever left the stems attached a note, too. It said something along the lines of seeing Jasmine out somewhere but not speaking, then noticing her shoes and promising to get closer to her the next time."

"Now, that is scary. I should reach out to Jasmine and see if she's okay."

"You know what else you should do?" Troy asked as the sleigh came to a stop in front of Cole's Sweet Shop. "Reach out to Dani and tell her about the podcast."

Chloe's eyes narrowed. She pointed toward the shop's antique wooden door. "Here comes the server with a tray of hot chocolate. Come on. Let's go grab some."

Her avoidance was all the response Troy needed. He followed her lead and climbed off the sleigh. After accepting a mug of steaming cocoa topped with whipped cream, he grabbed his cell and sent Chloe a text.

"I think my phone's going off," she said, unzipping her powder-blue jacket's pocket.

"It is. I just sent you a message."

"Why? I'm standing right here next to you."

"So that you'll have Dani's number. Just in case you change your mind and decide to contact her."

Chloe pulled the zipper back up. "Dani doesn't want to hear from me, Troy. Trust me. I've reached out to her several times over the years. Never once did I hear back."

"When was the last time you tried?"

"It's been a while."

"Respectfully, I think you should try again. Aside from the connection between your podcast and Jasmine's investigation, that friendship meant a lot to you both. It's a lot to just throw away. And now that you and I have reconnected, it seems like the right thing to do."

"Why? Because you're afraid of what Dani would say if she found out we've been talking behind her back?"

"Afraid?" Troy snorted. "No. Guilty? Maybe. And if I'm being honest, it pains me to see you two at odds. You all were like sisters."

"Were," Chloe muttered under her breath. "But fine. I'll think about it. Now, can we please drop it and enjoy the rest of our afternoon?"

"We sure can." Troy craned his neck, peering inside the bakery. "I'm going to try one of those hot chocolate croissants that were just pulled out of the oven. Would you like to indulge in one?"

"Yes, absolutely."

While Chloe began chatting about the last time she'd visited the resort, Troy replayed their conversation in his head. He contemplated telling Dani about the podcast himself.

Don't, he quickly resolved, realizing it'd be best to stay out of it. At least for the time being.

Considering how Chloe had already brushed past the topic, Troy knew she probably wouldn't be contacting Dani anytime soon. But eventually, one of them would have to say something.

Chapter Four

Dear Cece Speaks,

Greetings, my friend! My name is Gretchen Knight, and I am *Preyed Upon*'s biggest fan! I really love what you're doing and anxiously await every new episode. I bet I'm the first one tuning in the second they're posted! *Preyed Upon* has quickly become my absolute favorite true crime show. I am in awe of how hard you work considering I know firsthand all the research that goes into each episode. How, you ask? Because I have made NUMEROUS attempts to launch a podcast of my own. But things never seem to come together for me. You, on the other hand, hit the scene, and then, BOOM! You've already got a ton of subscribers! Kudos to you.

Hey, by the way, what's your real name? Cecilia? Celeste? Where are you from? What do you do for a living? I'm trying to figure out whether any of my guesses are correct. And one last question. Have you ever thought about bringing a cohost onto the show? If so, I'd love for you to consider me! And by consider, I mean hire me on the spot—lol! Just kidding. But not really…

Anyway, looking forward to hearing back from you

soon, Cece Speaks. In the meantime, I'll be biting my nails in anticipation of the next epi. Hope you have time to write me back today…

    XO,

    Gretchen

"Ugh," Chloe moaned before closing out of her email, then opening the Ratings and Reviews section of her last episode. Just as she'd expected, Gretchen had been the first listener to leave a comment. And per usual, it reeked of victim shaming.

> Another great episode, Cece Speaks! But COME ON! Why would Sinclair go out to some random bar alone, get drunk and start throwing ice at the other patrons?? On top of that, she walked home by herself after getting kicked out instead of calling a family member or friend to come and get her. How stupid! It's almost as if she was asking for something bad to happen to her. I'm honestly not surprised she was picked up by a crazed killer, then found stabbed to death on the side of the road. Ladies, you have GOT to start making better decisions!

"Too harsh, Gretchen," Chloe muttered before hiding the comment so that other listeners wouldn't see it. "Keep it up and you're gonna get yourself banned…"

Chloe had made it her business to record a disclaimer at the beginning of every episode, asking that listeners be kind and respectful. Yet Gretchen never adhered to the request. After every episode, there she was, leaving nasty remarks that always found the victim at fault.

The irritation swelling inside Chloe's chest shrank at the sight of all the five-star reviews and her growing list of followers. It was a pleasant surprise considering *Preyed Upon* had started off as a hobby to help fill a void.

Flipping open her notebook, she scanned the bullet points for her upcoming episode. It was the case of Trina Davenport, who had gone out on a date with a man she'd met through a dating app. Afterward she told him she wasn't interested. Instead of taking the news in stride, he pursued her relentlessly with endless phone calls and text messages. Trina went missing within two weeks of their date. Thirty-seven days later, she was found strangled to death in her car, which was parked haphazardly in the back of a grocery-store lot.

Chloe swiped open her phone and pulled up the Notes app in search of the killer's arrest date. Her thumb accidentally tapped the text-message app. Troy's thread was the first to appear. The last message he'd sent was the one with Dani's phone number attached.

The sight made her jaw clench, as did Troy's insistence that she call her. Deep down, Chloe knew he was right.

Just do it...

Before talking herself out of it, she dialed the number. Dani picked up on the first ring.

"This is Chief Miller."

Chloe gripped the side of her antique wooden desk, jerking in her chair as if a spring had popped.

"*Hello,* this is Chief Miller. How may I help you?"

She hadn't heard Dani's voice in years. It was still sweet and melodic, tinged with the slightest bit of rasp.

"Huh—hello…" Chloe stammered. "Hey, Dani. This is, um…this is Chloe."

Silence.

"Chloe Grant—"

"I know who you are, obviously," Dani snapped, her tone so brusque that she sounded like a completely different person. "What can I do for you?"

Grabbing a bottle of water, Chloe took a quick sip, then huffed a sharp inhalation. "I, uh…I was calling to tell you that I heard about those dead flower stems someone delivered to Jasmine Bailey's house."

She paused, waiting for Dani to respond. She was met with silence.

"Troy and I recently ran into one another," Chloe continued, "and I was telling him about a new project that I've launched."

A deep sigh swooshed through her ear. She remembered that sigh. It was the one Dani blew whenever she was annoyed as hell.

"You're calling to tell me about your podcast, is that correct? And the case you covered that's similar to what Jasmine experienced?"

Now it was Chloe's turn to go silent. Dani's cold, ultra-professional disposition was throwing her off. And if Troy had planned to report the incident to Dani himself, then why had he insisted that Chloe call her?

But she knew the answer. He'd wanted them to reconnect.

"*Chloe.* Are you still there?"

"Yes! Sorry, I'm here. I was just—I was just, um…"

"Listen, I'm gonna need for you to get on with it. I've got reports to review, trainings to schedule and a budget to approve. What is it that you need?"

"I need to talk to you," Chloe blurted before she could process what she was saying. "To ask how you're doing. Tell you I've moved back to Maxwell. And that I was almost killed back in Chicago."

Another deep sigh. Except this time, the irritation level seemed to have dropped a few decibels.

"Well, you calling out of the blue feels a bit strange considering you and I haven't spoken in forever."

And that's on you, Chloe wanted to reply. But she kept it to herself.

"But anyway," Dani continued, "I'm good. Welcome home. And I'm sorry to hear that you almost lost your life."

The last statement was laced with a soft sincerity, revealing hints of the old Dani. Chloe blinked back the tears that were teetering along the edges of her eyelids. "Thanks. I just wanted to make sure that you were aware of the connection between the incident at Jasmine's and my podcast."

"Yes, I am aware. Our police department is working hard to get to the bottom of who left the package. And as for your podcast, I doubt that there's any correlation between it and this incident. According to Troy, you haven't told many people about *Preyed Upon*. Isn't that correct?"

Chloe was slow to respond. She was too busy hanging on to the fact that Dani knew the name of her podcast. Had she listened to any of the episodes? Chloe was dying to ask. Back in the day, the ex-friends took on these types of endeavors together, rooting for one another along the way. Dani would've been on the journey with Chloe. Hearing her voice was a reminder of how much she missed those days.

"Is that correct?" Dani repeated a little louder.

"Yes, that's correct. Not too many people know I'm behind the podcast. Especially here in Maxwell. Except for you. And Troy, of course—"

"So," Dani interrupted, the phone rustling as if she were preparing to hang it up, "no one in town knows about it except for Troy and me. Obviously neither of us left the dead flower stems at Jasmine's house. You see where I'm going with this?"

Chloe winced at the cynicism in her voice. "I do. *Preyed Upon* probably isn't connected to the package. But I just wanted to make sure that you were aware of it. Now that I know you are, I'm good. So, um…yeah. I guess that's it."

"Okay, then. Well, my budget meeting is about to start. So if that's it, have a good day."

"Thanks. You—"

Before Chloe could say *too,* Dani disconnected the call.

"Hello?" she said, just to be sure. The other end of the line was silent.

She slid her phone across the desk, replaying the conversation in her head. So many years had passed since she and Dani had spoken. Chloe wished their first talk could've been more pleasant.

Crossing her arms over her chest, she contemplated calling Troy and asking why the hell he hadn't mentioned Dani knowing about *Preyed Upon.* The moment she grabbed her cell, it buzzed with a text notification from him.

"Speaking of the devil."

Hey, I was standing outside of Dani's office just now and overheard your convo. Glad you two spoke. Sounds like she isn't convinced the stems are connected to Preyed Upon. I'm starting to agree. We sent the package to the lab for testing. Hopefully something viable comes back. I'm about to sit in on Dani's budget meeting. Let's talk later.

Chloe sucked in a deep breath, reminding herself that Troy meant well. He just wanted to protect their town and reestablish the friendship. But after her conversation with Dani, it was clear that the chief wasn't interested in rekindling a thing. So if Troy brought it up again, Chloe would simply shut him down.

"This is so weird," Troy said, eyeing a photo on Chloe's phone screen.

It was late in the evening and he'd just arrived at her house. When she'd called thirty minutes prior, Troy had assumed Chloe was reaching out to discuss her conversation with Dani. But the panicked tremors in her voice said otherwise. As she began describing a strange text message she'd received, he'd decided to stop by and see it for himself.

"When did this come through again?" Troy asked.

"About an hour ago."

He enlarged the attachment. It was a video of him standing outside of Jasmine's house, unwrapping the dead flower stems.

"Are you *sure* you didn't ask someone from Maxwell PD to send that to me?" Chloe asked for the third time while fiddling with the drawstring on her fitted gray joggers.

"I'm positive. I never would've had someone send you this without alerting you first. Plus, it came from an anonymous number. No one on the team would've done that. So let's talk about who would have. And why."

She collapsed onto the couch, her gaze getting lost in the cream damask rug. "I wish I knew the answer to that, Troy. But I don't."

Sliding into the seat next to her, he replied, "Well, if you think about it, there were a few people back in Chicago who had a reason to get under your skin, right?"

"I would like to think that I left all the issues I had there behind me. I mean, if I was a problem, I'm gone now. I no longer work for the police department. Why would any of those people have reason to harass me?"

"I don't know. Revenge, maybe? They're holding a grudge that they can't let go of?"

"Could be. And now they're trying to get inside my head."

"What about your ex? You two weren't on the best of terms when things ended."

"We weren't. However, I did give him a call before I moved, letting him know I was leaving. We talked about our relationship. Our regrets. What we could've done differently. I thought we'd reached a place of understanding. I can't think of anything that would warrant him trying to get revenge all the way from the Midwest."

"But you never know," Troy said, typing bullet points from the conversation into his phone. "He did want you back and you rejected him. A man's ego can drive him to do some crazy things. And what about his current girlfriend? She started harassing you after they began dating, right?"

Chloe nodded, her fingernails digging into the sofa's textured teal fabric. "She did. And you know, come to think of it, Alex did email me a couple of weeks after I moved, asking how I was settling in. I didn't bother to respond. But I wonder if his girlfriend saw the message. That could have set her off."

"I'd hate to think that either of them would go to this extreme just to try and get back at you."

"Yeah, me too. But that woman was unhinged. She enjoyed going to great lengths to try and make me miserable. So did my ex-partner with the Chicago PD. His rage almost cost me my life."

"And with that being said, I'm adding all three of their names to my list of suspects. You know who else we should include? That writer you had issues with on *The Chicago Force*."

"Oh, for sure," Chloe agreed. "If you're making a list, he should definitely be on it."

"Okay, so we've got your ex Alex, his girlfriend Melissa, your ex-partner Justin and Simon the writer."

"Wait—how did you remember all those names?"

"Easy. I listen to everything you tell me."

A long stretch of silence passed between the pair. Chloe's gaze locked with Troy's as energy swirled between them.

There was an intensity behind her eyes. A longing that made him feel needed. Desired…

The buzzing inside his head snaked to his gut and stirred through his groin. Embarrassed, he tugged at the hem on his navy button-down shirt.

"You know, I could go for some coffee," Chloe said before standing. "Maybe with a shot of whiskey after the day I've had. Would you like a cup?"

"I'd love one. Thanks. When you come back, we can dig a little deeper into this list we made. Maybe run through which of these characters was most likely to have sent that text."

"Can I be honest with you?" she asked, stopping on the way to the kitchen.

"Of course."

"I'm exhausted. And I'd really like to table this discussion. At least for right now."

"Should we at least reach out to Dani and fill her in on this latest development?"

"We should. But not tonight. I need a minute to take all this in. Keep in mind I just left a hellish situation back in Chicago. I thought coming back home would be the answer. Just recently, life started to feel normal again. Good, even. I finally stopped running those traumatic experiences through my head over and over. You and I reconnected, which has been really nice. Then I just found out my latest podcast episode hit the charts."

"Really?" Troy asked, giving her a round of applause. "That's awesome, Chloe. Congratulations."

"Thank you. So, yeah, I just need a little time to let all this sink in. We've got our list. Plus, I'm sure Dani will still say that no one from Chicago would come all this way to retaliate against me."

"Not after she hears about this latest development," Troy rebutted, pointing toward Chloe's phone.

"We'll see."

He walked over and took her hand in his. "Well, I'll be keeping an eye on things. Just to make sure the situation doesn't escalate."

When she didn't respond, he braced himself for a debate.

"Okay," Chloe finally said, her fingertip gently caressing his palm. "Now, about that coffee. Are you sure you want me to add that shot of whiskey?"

"Positive," he murmured, struggling to keep his eyes off her backside as she sauntered into the kitchen.

Chapter Five

Chloe stood at the 221 trailhead of Sandstone Peak Mountain Preserve, adjusting the volume on her headphones.

"Wait—hold on," she said to Troy, whose robotic voice was breaking up on the other end of the phone. "The reception is terrible out here. I'm standing at the bottom of the trail. Isn't this where we're supposed to meet?"

"It is. That's what…trying to…you…"

"You're still breaking up. Listen, just send me a text and let me know how long you'll be. Hopefully it'll go through. I'll wait here for you."

Chloe disconnected the call and stared up at the sky, squinting at the blinding sunbeams peeking through the clouds. It was late afternoon, and she and Troy had made plans to hike one of Sandstone Peak's more moderate trails. The plan was to get a little exercise in while watching the sun set. But with Troy running late, she was hoping they wouldn't miss the height of the alpenglow.

It had been a week since he'd suggested she reach out to Dani and tell her about the text. But Chloe still hadn't drummed up the nerve to face her ex-friend again. Not after the chilly reception she'd received during their first conversation.

Maybe she was in denial. Despite the list of suspects Troy

and Chloe had compiled, she wasn't convinced someone from Chicago would go through the trouble of harassing her all the way in Arizona. And unless they'd done some extreme digging, none of them were aware of her connection to *Preyed Upon.*

Nevertheless, Chloe found comfort in knowing that Troy was keeping watch over her. He'd been spending more time at her place and checking in regularly. That, plus her Glock 22, gave her peace of mind.

Propping her foot against jagged gray siltstone, Chloe stretched her calf while pulling up podcast episode ideas on her phone.

1. Clarissa James: Drowned in a bathtub by her best friend, who then kidnapped her newborn baby
2. Ayanna Kincaid: Poisoned with oleander flowers by her husband of twenty-seven years
3. Star Renee: Stabbed to death by a fellow social media influencer/rival
4. Brooklyn Williams: Beaten to death by her college roommate

Chloe's head lurched when a text notification from Troy popped up on the screen.

I was saying that I'm held up at the station. Go on and start the hike without me. Don't want you to miss getting your pic of that amazing alpenglow. I should be leaving in about 30 minutes. I'll try and make it in time to meet you halfway at the Jasper Ridge trailhead.

Disappointment almost turned Chloe around and sent her back to the car. She'd been looking forward to the hike all week. Going at it alone would defeat the purpose of capturing that romantic sunset alongside—

What are you doing? Stop it...

Chloe pressed a knuckle against her temple. But the pressure didn't eliminate the images reeling through her mind. The ones she'd been envisioning for days. Visions of her walking closely beside Troy while climbing the sandy trails, underneath the stunning pink- and lavender-painted sky. Taking selfies among the red rock landscapes, with gently rolling foothills and lush greenery serving as their backdrop.

Intimate thoughts of Troy were becoming an everyday occurrence. Slowly, they'd transformed into actual feelings, thumping inside her chest. Tamping them down had been a challenge. If Troy's flirtatious winks, lingering stares and affectionate touches were any indication of where he stood, the feelings were mutual.

But it wasn't just sexual tension driving their connection. The bond was rooted in comfort. And security. Troy was her safe space. With him, she could vent freely about anything. Chloe served the same purpose as he shared the challenges of being a rookie cop in their hometown. Having to show deference to people he'd grown up with. Working for his sister and readjusting to small-town living. She understood the shift in dynamics and lack of anonymity. The expectations. The mundane pace. The feeling of starting over.

There was, however, one thing standing in the way of their bond blossoming into something more—Dani. Her disdain toward Chloe was palpable, even over the phone. She'd never approve of her and Troy getting together. With his family dynamic and job on the line, Chloe wondered if he'd be willing to take the risk.

She glanced around the trailhead, hoping he would surprise her by showing up earlier than expected. But Troy was nowhere in sight.

As she set off on the trail, Chloe opened her music app and tapped the '90s hip-hop workout playlist. Her thoughts shifted back to the potential podcast episodes. After running through the list once again, she settled on Brooklyn Williams, the victim who'd been beaten to death by her college roommate.

Chloe turned off the music and pulled up the Voice Memos app, then began dictating everything she knew so far about the case.

"Brooklyn was a junior at Sowell University in Charlotte, North Carolina, when she was murdered. She'd been living off campus at the Blue Ridge Apartments complex. Her roommate, Tanya Osborne, was a transfer student who'd befriended Brooklyn after they began playing tennis together on the university's team."

There was a bounce in Chloe's step as she climbed. It wasn't just the excitement of working on her passion project. It was knowing she'd be seeing Troy soon.

A group of hikers appeared up ahead. Chloe stopped recording and stepped to the side as the trail narrowed.

"Happy hiking!" one of the men called out on the way down. "Enjoy that sunset!"

"I will, thanks! You're not sticking around for it?"

"No, we're exhausted. We've been out here all day. Time to rest up and grab some food."

"Gotcha," Chloe said with a wave.

She peered up the pathway in search of other hikers. While voices echoed in the distance, no one emerged. That wasn't surprising. Weekdays on the trail, along with cooler fall mountain temperatures, meant fewer trekkers.

Glancing at the time on her phone, she saw that she'd been

climbing for almost twenty minutes. Troy would be there soon, probably coming up the backside of the mountain to reach Jasper Ridge Trail quicker. Chloe was taking the scenic route. She didn't want to miss the first phase of the sunset.

A chilly breeze rattled the collar on her bright purple windbreaker. She pulled the zipper up to her chin, tapped the record button on her cell and continued climbing.

"Once Brooklyn and Tanya moved in together, they grew even closer. According to fellow classmates, the pair did everything together. From partying and working out to eating meals and joining a sorority, they were inseparable. But then Brooklyn began dating the school's star basketball player, Joseph Freedman. And that's when her and Tanya's friendship took a turn for the worse."

Boom!

Chloe's gray Salomon sneakers skidded over a rotting stump. She ducked down, backing against a siltstone rock formation.

"What the *hell* was that?" she whispered.

No one was around to answer.

Her heart rate elevated as she struggled to catch her breath. Chloe blamed it on the higher altitude. Deep down, she knew it was fear.

Calm down. Everything's fine...

Just for good measure, she remained rooted against the rugged mountainside for several seconds. All was still and peaceful. A stone had probably fallen onto the trail.

It could've been Chloe's PTSD that had her thinking irrationally. Seeing things that weren't there and creating catastrophic scenarios in her head. She was still raw from the incident back in Chicago. Sudden movements, abrupt surprises...any unexpected occurrence sent her over the edge.

Deep breaths. Keep going...

Squaring her shoulders, Chloe continued up the path. Once several minutes of uninterrupted peace ticked by, she continued recording Brooklyn's story.

"While Tanya had a problem with Brooklyn's boyfriend spending the night at their apartment, Brooklyn refused to compromise. She felt as though she could do as she pleased since she was paying half the rent. This led to Tanya throwing fits over a slew of issues, both big and small. She'd complain that Brooklyn wasn't cleaning up after herself. That she'd used her things and eaten her food without permission. Noise complaints soon followed, with Tanya insisting that Brooklyn and Joseph played their music too loudly. Again, the couple refused to compromise and even began throwing parties without notifying Tanya beforehand. When a gold bangle bracelet that she'd been gifted by her parents went missing, Tanya filed a police report, accusing Brooklyn, Joseph or one of their guests of stealing it."

Chloe stopped at a fork in the trail. Two signs were planted in the middle. Marble Rock Trail was to her right. Gravel Ghost Trail was to her left. There was no sign pointing her in the direction of Jasper Ridge Trail.

She spun around in search of another post. There wasn't one.

"Nooo," she moaned, pressing her hand against her forehead. "Girl, what have you done?"

But Chloe knew exactly what she'd done. Between thoughts of Troy and dictating Brooklyn's story, she had made a wrong turn.

She swiped open the web browser and attempted to pull up Sandstone Peak's website. The screen went white as the loading icon froze. No reception.

"Damn it!"

Chloe contemplated making her way back down the trail

in hopes of running into Troy. But the missed pathway had completely turned her around. She'd be better off trying her luck meeting him at Jasper Ridge. Convinced her instincts would lead her in the right direction, Chloe made a left onto Gravel Ghost Trail and prayed it would lead her there.

The path's terrain was rougher than the one she'd just hiked. Narrower, too. If she were to encounter fellow climbers, Chloe didn't know whether there would be enough room to pass.

"Just worry about what's in front of you right now," she said aloud, talking to herself in hopes of keeping her cool.

Dusk was beginning to settle over the landscape. The sky's orange and red hues were fading into deep shades of purplish-gray. An urgency tingled along the soles of Chloe's feet. Shallow puffs of the desert air dried her throat as she climbed the gravelly earth. A long sip of water would've been nice. But she'd been so excited to meet up with Troy that she'd left her Hydro Flask in the car.

Chloe was in desperate need of a distraction. So she hit the record button and continued dictating podcast notes.

"The police report Tanya filed against Brooklyn and her boyfriend marked the end of their friendship. After that, it was war between the roommates. Law enforcement was called to the apartment numerous times due to verbal and physical attacks. Brooklyn eventually agreed to ban Joseph from visiting. But by then, it was too late. In Tanya's eyes, Brooklyn had gone too far—"

Bzzz!

The buzz of her cell sent Chloe stumbling toward the side of the cliff.

"You have *got* to calm down!" she told herself before swiping open the home screen. No new calls appeared in the log. There were no unread texts or emails, either.

"No damn reception…"

Holding the phone high in the air, Chloe pivoted, desperate to pick up a signal-strength bar. No luck. So she kept going.

"Getting revenge on Brooklyn became an obsession for Tanya. She began harassing her and making outlandish claims, even accusing Brooklyn of drugging her. When confronted, Tanya snapped. A fight broke out between the former friends. According to Tanya, Brooklyn slapped her in the face, prompting Tanya to grab the nearest weapon—her tennis racket. She hit Brooklyn in the head with it repeatedly until she fell unconscious. Brooklyn never woke up from the attack. Once paramedics and the medical examiner arrived, she was declared dead on the scene."

"Hey! Ay…ay…ay…"

Chloe jumped at the sound of a gruff male voice bouncing against the mountainside.

Troy? she almost yelled back. *Is that you?*

But she didn't. Because it might not have been him.

A quick scan of the area didn't reveal any fellow hikers. It was clear that Gravel Ghost was the trail less traveled. Which was why Chloe decided to get the hell off of it.

She spun around and shot back down the path. A gust of frigid wind pushed her forward, causing the soles of her sneakers to skate over a cluster of jagged rocks.

Stay on your feet!

Visions of falling on the trail filled her head. Twisting her ankle. Being unable to move with no cell reception and no water. Once it grew dark, no one would be able to find her—

"Stop it!" Chloe hissed, angry that she'd slipped back into the catastrophic thinking.

"I see youuu…"

Chloe stopped. Wondered if she was hearing things again. But no. Not this time. Those three words had crept through the air like an evil spirit, whistling in the wind. Yet there wasn't a soul in sight.

It's just your imagination. It's just your imagination...

The affirmation swirled inside her head over and over again, right along with flashbacks of that night at the Righteous Nation's headquarters. The attack. Being let down by her fellow officers. Retiring early, then returning home to Maxwell, only to be haunted by all she'd left behind.

"Aye, you!" someone croaked. "Stop right there!"

There was no denying it. That husky, sinister voice was not a figment of her imagination. Nor did it belong to Troy.

Chloe picked up speed, practically skiing down the gritty trail. The peak of the alpenglow had eluded her as dusk continued to invade the scene. The lush greenery she'd enjoyed on the way up transformed into haunting shadows on the way down. She flew past a sign that read Jasper Ridge Trail. Its arrow pointed to the left. But Chloe was in no mood to hit another pathway. She just wanted to get the hell off the mountain.

Her phone rang. The shrill jingle sent her stumbling dangerously close to the edge. She caught herself, fumbling to silence the phone in the event she was being followed.

"Hello?" she rasped.

"Hey, it's Troy. I've been trying to call and text you. But I guess the reception is bad up there and—"

"Where *are* you?"

"I'm in the parking lot. I tried to get here as soon as I could. I'm mad I missed the sunset. Can I make it up to you by—"

"Listen to me, Troy," Chloe interrupted. "I think somebody's following me."

"Hold on. You're breaking up. Say that again?"

"I think somebody is following me!" she repeated through

panicked huffs of air. "I'm hearing weird voices. Like someone's calling out to me or something."

"Did you see anybody?"

"No. And that's what's so weird. I could hear them. But I couldn't see them."

"Are you sure? Because I just saw a big group of teenagers going up the main trail not too long ago. Maybe you heard them talking to each other."

The news gave her a slight bit of relief. But she wouldn't fully relax until she was back at the trailhead.

"Are you still up at Jasper Ridge Trail?" he asked. "Because I can come up and meet you—"

"No, I never made it there. I missed the entrance and ended up on Gravel Ghost Trail."

"How did that happen? That trail isn't easy to get to and no one really hikes it."

"Yeah, I just learned that the hard way."

"Listen, I can tell you're shaken up. Do you want me to come up and meet you?"

Chloe peered toward the bottom of the mountain. "Do me a favor. Wave your arms in the air."

"I'm waving. Can you see me?"

"I can! I'm coming to you now."

It took forever to finally make it back down. Troy jogged over, pulling her into his arms.

"Are you good?" he asked.

"I am now."

"Are you hungry?"

"I'm starving."

"Me too. Why don't we go grab dinner and you can tell me all about the voices you heard chirping through the mountains?"

"See, you're cracking jokes, but I know what I heard!"

Warmth radiated throughout her entire body when he slid his hand along the small of her back and led her to the parking lot.

"How does barbecued salmon and loaded baked potatoes from Autumn's Den sound?" he asked.

"That sounds perfect."

"Cool." He opened her car door and helped her inside. "Follow me there?"

"Yep. I'll be right behind you."

Chloe watched as Troy walked away, his strong, confident swagger righting every wrong that had just occurred.

The second they pulled out of the lot, her phone buzzed. She could see Troy staring at her in the rearview mirror. Chloe gave him a nod and grabbed her phone, already smiling before reading the text.

It was so nice seeing your beautiful face glowing against the Sandstone Peak sunset. Sorry we didn't get a chance to meet. I certainly tried. But that damn trail got the best of me. No worries, though. We will next time...

Chloe's grin shriveled into a curve of confusion. She checked for a phone number. There wasn't one. The message had been sent anonymously.

She closed out the message and called Troy.

"Hey," he said. "What's up?"

"I just got the weirdest text. At first I thought it was from you. But apparently it's from someone who saw me out on the trail."

"Really? You don't recognize the number?"

"No. It was sent anonymously, just like the other one."

"Ugh," Troy groaned. "I'll check it out when we get to the restaurant."

A FLASH OF sadness flickered across Chloe's eyes. Her head swiveled toward the English brick fireplace. Troy waited for her to turn back. Make eye contact. Indulge him in a little conversation. But she didn't. Instead her gaze remained lost in the dancing flame's orange glow.

Her mood was a complete contradiction of the guests seated around them. The rustic wooden tables inside Autumn's Den were filled with gleeful diners, laughing and toasting over plates of succulent steaks, spicy fish tacos and slices of home-made pie. Troy had suggested they dine there for the warm, intimate vibes. But after receiving that text, Chloe seemed ready to crawl into bed and hide underneath the covers.

"So you think that message is linked to the same person who sent the photo of the dead flower stems?" Troy asked.

"Absolutely. Without a doubt in my mind."

"And you still don't want to have a sit-down with Dani to discuss all this?"

She hesitated, swallowing down the last of her lemon drop martini before replying, "No. Or not yet, at least. Not until I have a more solid lead for her to go off. Especially after that last conversation we had."

"This is different, Chloe. This is about your safety. It's not like you're trying to hash out the past or rekindle your friendship. Not that there's anything wrong with that, but..."

"I'd rather try and figure this out on my own. With your help, of course. Let's not forget I'm a former detective. Once I get some answers, I'll talk to Dani."

"And why are you waiting again?"

"Because I don't want to go to her with something she might deem frivolous. I mean, it's not like I'm being threat-ened. The messages are just strange, that's all."

Troy rattled the ice in his whiskey glass, then slipped a cube into his mouth. He needed something to shut himself up. To stop him from insisting Chloe do something she clearly didn't want to do. If she didn't think the texts posed a threat, then he had to respect that.

He watched as she picked at the sugar coating the rim of her glass. Judging by the tremor in her fingers, she wasn't completely convinced.

Their day wasn't supposed to turn out like this. He should've been out there on that trail with her, snapping pictures and enjoying the stunning sunset. The reports could've waited. But he couldn't tell Dani he had plans. Not this time. She would have slipped into scuba mode and taken a deep dive into his personal life. After working alongside her all day, he wasn't in the mood to lie. Plus, if she had arched her right brow and given him a prying smirk, that might have pulled the truth right out of him.

"Thanks again for dinner," Chloe said. "The salmon here is still one of my favorite dishes in town."

It was the third time she'd thanked him. Troy figured that was her way of changing the subject. So he obliged. "Yep, mine, too. And you're welcome. It's the least I could do after missing that sunset with you."

Chloe's face fell. She turned her cell over so that the screen faced the table. He regretted bringing up the hike, as it was a reminder of the strange text.

"How are you two doing over here?" the server asked. "Would you like refills on your drinks? Or how about a delicious piece of homemade—"

"No, thank you," Chloe interrupted through a pleasant but tired smile. "We'll just take the check."

"Yes, ma'am. I'll be right back."

Yep, she's had it. With this day and with me...

Disappointment ripped through Troy's gut as he pulled out his wallet. He'd hoped Chloe would be up for stopping by one of his favorite jazz spots for some live music and another round of cocktails. But judging by her dismal demeanor, she was ready to call it a night.

"So, um…" he began, almost afraid to say what he was thinking. "I can't really consider this a makeup dinner since you weren't really up for it. I'd love to get together again soon. You know, so that I can *really* make it up to you."

Chloe leaned against the side of her burgundy leather chair, perking up a bit. "Sure. I'd like that. Maybe we can try something a little less adventurous next time, though."

"You got it," he replied when the response was barely out of her mouth. "We can do whatever you'd like."

After paying the bill, he walked Chloe to her car. Even though they'd made plans to hang out again, Troy was having a hard time letting her leave. "Are you sure you're ready to go home? Even if you don't want to stay out, we could go back to my place and listen to some music, have a couple more drinks…"

"As much as I'd love to, I really am exhausted. But I promise to take you up on that rain check."

He restrained the sigh simmering in his chest and opened her door. "No worries. I understand."

That was what Troy's mouth said. But if it were up to him, they'd continue enjoying each other's company into the early morning hours…

Chapter Six

Chloe pulled to the curb a good distance away from Jasmine's house, not wanting to get entangled in all the emergency vehicles parked out front. Almost half the block had been cordoned off. Inquisitive neighbors stood in front of their homes, shivering against the cool night air while watching the hectic scene. Red and blue lights flashed from the back of the ambulance and tops of cop cars, transforming the dark street into a chaotic blur of color. Jasmine's family stood along the edge of yellow caution tape hanging between two desert ironwood trees, doubled over in tears while clinging to one another.

Chloe's body shuddered at the sight. It triggered memories of her days in Chicago, pulling up to violent crime scenes as bloody bodies lay sprawled on the ground. Blood poured from gunshot and stab wounds as life drained from the victims' eyes. Processing murder scenes had been the toughest part of the job.

But what had occurred at Jasmine's house that evening was something different. Something personal. An indirect attack against Chloe.

Her phone buzzed. It was a text from Troy.

Are you almost here?

I just pulled up. I'll grab my evidence collection kit in case you need me to jump in and help, then meet you out front.

Willing her trembling legs to carry her, Chloe made her way toward Jasmine's house. She gripped the kit tighter. The scene blurred as she got closer. Dread weighted her feet at the thought of having to see Jasmine's dead body.

"Hey," Troy said as she approached. "Thanks for coming out—"

"What is she doing here?"

Chloe winced at the disgust in Dani's voice.

"I asked her to come," Troy confirmed.

"Why?"

"Because I thought we could use her expertise. It's not like Maxwell PD is faced with murder investigations on a regular basis."

"Nice to know you've got so much faith in your squad," Dani shot back. "Not to mention, if Chloe wanted to work for the Maxwell PD? She had her chance."

Chloe stood tall, attempting to appear unfazed while she scrambled for a rebuttal.

"Chief Miller, please," Troy said. "Can you just let her take a look at the body? The more sets of eyes we've got on the scene, the better. Isn't that what you always say?"

Dani's glare shifted from Troy to Chloe, then down to her crime scene kit. Before she could respond, Chloe threw a hand in the air.

"Excuse me, Chief Miller, but I'm just here to help. Not get in the way of the investigation or challenge your authority. Plus, I think this murder might be connected to me."

Chloe paused, waiting for some sort of response. Dani remained silent.

"Come on, Chief," she pleaded. "Jasmine was a friend of mine. And I'd really like to assist you in getting to the bottom of this."

Propping a fist on her hip, Dani turned to Troy. Wrinkles

formed around her mouth as her jaw clenched with disdain. It was clear she was on the verge of telling her brother off. But Troy didn't bend. He glared right back at her.

"Let me ask you this," he finally said. "How many murders have you investigated?"

"Officer Miller, please don't ask me questions you already know the answer to."

"So none, correct?" he continued before pointing at Chloe. "And how many murders have *you* investigated?"

"I, um, I'm not sure," she stammered, despite the real answer being more than she could count. "But it's been quite a few."

"Hey, Chief!" an officer called out from Jasmine's front yard. "Could you come and take a look at this?"

"I'll be right there!"

Troy nudged Dani's shoulder. "So, are we good? Can Chloe give us a hand?"

"Fine," Dani barked before pointing at her. "Just make sure you stay out of the way. And I know you're a former hotshot Chicago detective and all, but please stick to your word and don't try and take over my crime scene. That is, if sticking to your word is something you can handle."

Chloe's back stiffened at the jab. But her poker face remained in place as she replied, "That won't be a problem, Chief Miller. Thank you."

A few moments passed. Chloe remained planted in her spot on the pavement, waiting for Dani to take her to the body. But the chief hesitated, her feet shuffling as if she was figuring out her next move.

"Yeah, and, uh…" Dani muttered, seemingly more to herself than anyone else. "I appreciate you coming out."

The comment almost knocked Chloe off her feet. Just

when she was beginning to formulate the words *you're wel-come*, Dani jogged back toward the scene.

"That was…strange," Chloe said while following Troy toward the front gate.

"You call it strange. I call it a step in the right direction. I'm just glad you're here."

"Yeah, me too."

Chaos surrounded the area as first responders swarmed the house. Neighbors were being questioned on the outskirts while officers' dizzying flashlights beamed in every direction. Loud voices rattled Chloe's ears, sending her into a state of confusion.

Keep calm. You've got this…

"Hey," Troy said, gently nudging her arm. "You all right?"

"I am," she lied. "It's just been a minute since I've been at a crime scene. And this is the first one I've worked where the victim was a friend."

"I'm so sorry. I didn't even think about that. Maybe I shouldn't have asked you to—"

"No," Chloe interrupted. "You did the right thing by asking me to come out. It wouldn't feel right not being a part of this investigation."

"Listen, I apologize for the way Dani reacted to you being here. But at least the conversation ended on a semipositive note."

"If that's what you wanna call it. You probably should've asked Dani if it was okay for me to be here instead of just having me show up, though, don't you think? Because I never would've come had I known you didn't clear it with her first."

"I know. Which is exactly why I kept it to myself. I figured everything would work out once you got here. And what do you know? My plan worked."

The debate ended as Jasmine's body, covered in a white

sheet, came into view. Emotions were brushed to the side. Chloe's mind shifted into work mode.

"Is the medical examiner here yet?" she asked.

"No, and he should've been here by now. I'll check in with Dani and find out his ETA."

Chloe stood in the driveway and pulled on a protective mask and gloves, then slipped a pair of booties over her combat boots. A long breath of air rushed her lungs. She blew it out slowly through tight lips, staring at the porch where Jasmine's body lay.

"You sure you're up for this?" Troy asked.

"I'm positive. Can I take a look at the body?"

"Of course."

Chloe tried to ignore the throbbing in her head as officers breezed past them. Bracing herself, she followed Troy up the porch steps.

Hold it together. Hold it together...

When he pulled back the sheet, Chloe almost fell to her knees. Blood had pooled underneath Jasmine's body, soaking her yellow sweatshirt and yoga pants. Her arms were splayed at her sides. Her legs were bent awkwardly, and one furry slipper covered only her right foot.

What jarred Chloe to the core was Jasmine's facial expression. The terror in her wide eyes. The curve in her gaping mouth. Her pale skin. The deep burgundy bruise on her left cheek.

"Any guess as to how this happened?" Chloe rasped.

"We started off examining the chest area, which at first glance appeared to be the source of the bleeding. There were several puncture wounds consistent with a sharp object. I'm guessing it was a knife, considering their slim triangular shape. Neighbors reported hearing piercing screams. But they didn't hear gunshots."

Chloe turned away. "I'm gonna take a look around the area," she said over her shoulder, neglecting to add that she could no longer look at Jasmine lying there lifeless.

"I'll join you."

She was glad for the company, as she didn't want to be alone. Pulling a flashlight from her kit, she made her way up and down the driveway, searching the stones for evidence.

A faint marking near a line of Belgian blocks caught her eye. Moving in closer, she shone her light on the stain. Half of a bloody shoe print was embedded in the rocks.

Pulling a gelatin lifter from her kit, she said, "I think I've got something here."

"What is that? A shoe impression?"

"Looks like it."

"Good catch." Troy crouched down next to her, flashing his light toward the print. "Judging by the lines and curves in that lug pattern, it could be the sole of a Timberland boot. Men's size twelve or thirteen, maybe?"

"Possibly. We'll find out once I lift the print and you send it to the crime lab." Chloe took several photos, then peeled the adhesive off the back of the lifter. "Question. When did the last murder occur here in Maxwell?"

"Hmm. I believe it was a little over twenty years ago."

"That's what I thought—"

Words caught in Chloe's throat as she removed the adhesive, then placed the gelatin side over the impression. Pressing her fingertip across the lift, she whispered, "This is my fault."

"Chloe, please. Come on. Why would you say that? You and Jasmine hadn't been in touch in recent years, had you? You have no idea what she was into, or *who* she was into, or—"

"Listen to me. This is my fault. You know about the podcast episode involving the dead floral stems."

"I do. I actually listened to it. And I don't remember hearing anything remotely similar to what happened to Jasmine tonight."

"Well, you must not have listened to part two. That's when I talked about how the victim was found stabbed to death on her front porch."

Troy was slow to respond. He nodded, his wide eyes still on the gelatin lifter clinging to the print.

"Okay," he finally muttered. The beam from his flashlight swung back and forth. "So what are you saying?"

Chloe couldn't find the words. Not yet. "What do you think?"

"What do *I* think? I think you should stop blaming yourself for this. Murders happen every day. The world is changing, and Maxwell isn't what it used to be."

"Did you notice the bruise on Jasmine's left cheek?"

"I did."

"Were you or any of the other officers able to make out what may have caused it?"

"At first glance it looked like a bite mark. But of course we'll have to wait on the medical examiner's report before that can be confirmed."

Shooting to her feet, Chloe asked, "Wanna hear something ironic?"

"I'm listening."

"The victim I covered on *Preyed Upon* who received the dead stems? She was found stabbed to death on her front porch. With a deep bite mark on her left cheek."

"And you spoke on that in your latest episode?"

"I did."

Waving his arms in the air, Troy yelled, "Chief Miller! Hey, anyone know where the chief went?"

"Troy, no! Not now. Dani's overwhelmed enough as it is. Let her get through today and I'll take this to her later."

"*Later* meaning…"

"Soon," she blurted, despite not being ready for a face-to-face with her former best friend at any point in the near future.

Chapter Seven

Chloe stood stoically in the back of Blackman Funeral Home's basement, fanning her face with Jasmine's obituary. She'd struggled to hold back tears throughout the entire service. When she and Troy headed downstairs for repast, she'd assumed a bit of the emotional burden would lift. It hadn't.

A combination of guilt and grief weighed on her spirit. The loss hurt. Chloe carried the burden of *Preyed Upon* being partly to blame. At the same time she, along with Troy and the rest of Maxwell PD, was feeling the pressure to solve the case.

"It's so weird," Troy whispered, "the thought of a killer attending their victim's funeral, isn't it?"

"It is. But it's more common than you think. I attended victims' funerals all the time back in Chicago. Oftentimes the killers would be right there among the family members, mourning as if they were so hurt. It's like they got a kick out of observing the aftermath of what they'd done."

"That's pitiful. And plausible, all at the same time. You know what else is weird? Working during a funeral. I'm trying to be discreet, but I've got my eyes and ears wide-open. Has anybody caught your attention yet?"

Chloe scanned the quaint room, its soft lighting, sheer drapes and plush jewel-toned furniture setting a comforting tone amid the somber environment. A man she'd been watching since he arrived at the viewing approached the buffet table. He was almost handsome, his pinched baby face appearing familiar.

"Yes," she said, discreetly nodding in the man's direction. "That guy."

"Which guy?"

"The one in the tight pewter suit with the linebacker shoulders and balding head. You see him? Sticking his face inside every chafing dish?"

"Thanks to that extremely specific description you just gave, yes. I see him."

"If I'm not mistaken, that's Darren Simmons. He and Jasmine dated during high school and her freshman year of college. I'm sure you remember him being a star football player during his time at Cooper's High. He went to college on a full scholarship and was a shoo-in for the NFL. He was actually drafted by the Seattle Seahawks. But he tore his Achilles during practice before the season started, then refused to follow the doctor's rehab orders. That injury ended his career before it even started."

"Oh, yeah, I remember Darren. I'd already moved to LA by the time he left Seattle and came back to Maxwell. I didn't recognize him with the extra weight he's put on. But now that you've run down his résumé, tell me. What seems suspicious about him?"

"Well, when he and Jasmine dated, Darren was pretty possessive of her. To the point where her parents and the school principal had to get involved. All his incessant phone calls and text messages, monitoring her social media, trying to regulate who she could and couldn't talk to, things like that. It got so bad that her mother wanted to ask for an order of protection. But Jasmine talked her out of it."

"Did he ever get physical with her?"

"Once," Chloe said, dipping her head toward her cup of fruit punch when Darren looked their way. "When she told him she wasn't going to attend the University of Arizona with him. He choked her until she almost passed out. That got him a couple of nights in jail. Jasmine refused to press charges, so that's as far as it went. She was so scared of him that she didn't break things off until second semester of freshman year, after the football fame and sports groupies went to his head."

"Now it makes sense why no one's been talking to him. Do you really think he could have something to do with Jasmine's murder?"

"Right now I'm not putting anything past anybody. But the thing is, whoever left those dead flower stems at Jasmine's house, then killed her, seems to have something against me, too. Darren and I never had any beef. At least, as far as *I* know we didn't. I always kept my distance and tried to stay out of their drama."

"Well, time will tell. I'll be interested to see if we get any hits on the evidence that was collected at the scene."

"If any of it's viable," Chloe contended. "Don't forget, they were all partials. The fingerprints, the shoe print...not the best quality. But the good news is Darren's fingerprints should be stored in the FBI's national fingerprint database, because last I heard, he owns a tow truck business."

"Good to know. That means we'll have something to compare them to if—"

Troy stopped abruptly, his head jerking in the other direction.

"What's wrong?" Chloe asked.

"I think Darren's heading this way."

"Oh, no. I am not in the mood to talk to him."

"Well, get ready. Because here he—"

"Hey, Chloe Grant!" Darren boomed, almost knocking her against the wall when he went in for a hug. "Long time, no see! Did you move back to Maxwell? I thought you were living in New York!"

She straightened the cap sleeves on her black crepe knit dress, then stepped aside, releasing herself from his clumsy embrace. "Yes, I did move back. And I was actually living in Chicago."

"That's right! You were working for the Chicago PD and acting on that show, *The Chi-Town Squad*."

Chloe didn't bother to correct him, instead asking, "So what have you been up to these days?"

"You know, just grinding. Struggling to keep my towing company from going under. Urging my wife to stop spending so much money and go get a job. Begging my twin boys to pick up a football instead of a tennis racket. Wishing I could go back to the day I blew out my Achilles so I could run that play differently and live out the life I was *supposed* to live. But hey, look on the bright side. Things could always be worse. I could be where Jasmine is right now."

The crass statement sent Chloe rocking back on her black suede heels. As her eyes squinted in disgust, Troy swooped in and extended a hand.

"I don't believe we've met. Formally, at least. I'm Troy. Troy Miller."

Darren's grip almost swayed Troy's entire body from side to side. "Oh, yeah. I know you. You're Dani's little brother. How's she doing?"

"She's doing great. I'm sure you heard the news that she took over as Maxwell's chief of police."

"I did, I did. Good for her."

Droplets of sweat popped up along Darren's receding hairline. He attempted to shove his hands inside his pockets, but his tight pants wouldn't allow it.

"Is Dani here?" he mumbled, spinning an awkward 360-degree turn.

"No, she paid her respects yesterday during the visitation. The family understands she's busy working the case, which is of the utmost importance to us. So I'm here representing the Millers."

"Gotcha, gotcha. That makes sense. Makes total sense…"

"Were you and Jasmine still in touch before her murder?" Chloe asked.

An uncomfortable silence fell over the group. She didn't care. Her detective instincts had kicked in, as did her memory of how badly Darren's behavior affected her friend.

"We, um…yuh—yeah, sort of," he stammered. "Well, not really—"

"Which is it? Were you two in touch or not?"

"Damn, what is this? Some kind of interrogation?" he replied before shooting off a howling chuckle.

When neither Chloe nor Troy cracked a smile, Darren straightened up. "I wouldn't say we were in touch, per se. I'd send her the occasional direct message over Instagram every now and then or whatever. And she'd respond. Sometimes…"

"Did your wife know you'd been reaching out to her?" Troy asked.

The question left Darren's lower lip flailing. Several moments passed before he finally muttered, "No. She didn't. But it wasn't even like that. I was just checking in with an old friend to see how she was doing. That's all. And I already know where you're going with this. The answer is no. I did not have anything to do with Jasmine's murder."

"We weren't insinuating that you did," Chloe shot back.

"Yeah, okay. Whatever you say." He glanced down at his

watch while backing away. "And on that note, I think it's time for me to get outta here. I've got some, uh…some things I need to take care of. Good seeing you two."

"You as well," Chloe replied through tightened lips.

Both she and Troy watched as he jogged toward the exit.

"We need to find out where Darren was the night Jasmine was killed," Chloe declared.

Chapter Eight

Chloe pulled into the driveway, glancing over her shoulder before putting the car in Park. She couldn't make out much, as dusk had already settled and the streetlamps had yet to come on.

The sky had gone from a vibrant shade of blue to a bleak, sunless gray, casting an eerie blanket of darkness across the scenic cul-de-sac. Dread simmered in Chloe's gut as she envisioned their suspect lunging from the yellow creosote bushes lining her town house. She couldn't seem to turn off the torturous scenarios. Her mind had been playing endless tricks on her. Tricks that never came to fruition. Yet her trembling hand still hovered over the start-engine button, hesitant to turn off the car in case she had to make a quick getaway.

Since Jasmine's murder, Chloe rarely went out at night anymore. At least, not by herself. But today, time seemed to fly by while she was running errands. Stopping to chat with old acquaintances had set her back at least an hour. The sun set sooner than she'd expected. It had been a race against time to beat the darkness home—one that Chloe lost.

Just call Troy...

But she was apprehensive. Chloe didn't want him to know just how uneasy she felt simply getting out of the car. Plus, he'd be there as soon as he left the station. With the investigation in full swing, she couldn't expect him to be by her side 24/7.

"You're being ridiculous," Chloe muttered. "Just get out of the car and go inside the house."

Deep breaths failed to steady her erratic heart rate. Maxwell's murderer had left her paranoid, to the point where her head was on a constant swivel. She'd thought the days of living dangerously were behind her after leaving Chicago. Never did she expect a killer to descend upon her hometown—emulating her podcast, no less—a fact that left Chloe feeling as though she could be next.

For weeks she'd been plagued by thoughts of being watched and followed, leaving her on the verge of unraveling. The only time she felt the slightest sense of relief was when Troy was by her side. But in moments like this, she had only herself, her Glock and her police training for protection. That should've been good enough. Yet it wasn't. The day her Chicago PD unit left her hanging inside the Righteous Nation's headquarters ravaged any real sense of security. No amount of training or weaponry could override her fear once it penetrated her mind.

Fight through it. Do not let this situation get the best of you.

The affirmation was enough for her to turn off the engine and open the door. But the moment Chloe's combat boot hit the pavement, her muscles cramped with uncertainty. Something didn't feel right. What that something was, she didn't know.

All was quiet on the block. A few neighbors' porch lights were on, but there wasn't much activity happening in front of their houses or along the sidewalks. The calm should've been peaceful. Yet it wasn't. The stillness was unsettling. Jarring, even.

Slamming the car door behind her, Chloe made a run for

the porch. Her feet pounded the limestone stairs. But when she hit the ledge and reached for her keys, they weren't in her hand.

Damn it!

She could've sworn she'd grabbed them out of her purse before leaving the car. Her fixation on being attacked had drowned out reality. Frustration clenched her jaws as she dug inside the bag. When metal edges scraped against her palm, she grabbed the ring, struggling to control her trembling hand as she rammed the key inside the lock.

Chloe jolted when her car's shining headlights went out, shrouding her in complete darkness. She hadn't left any lights on, thinking she'd be back home before dark. The key jammed inside the lock while the dizzying buzz of cicadas rattled her eardrums. Awful images of someone pouncing from behind and taking her down came rushing back. But a quick glance over her shoulder proved once again that it was all in her head.

The click of the lock gave Chloe a slight sense of ease. She pushed through the door, practically falling into the living room. Her shoulder rammed the frame in the process. Relief overrode the pain. She'd made it inside in one piece.

Within seconds, Chloe had the door bolted and every light turned on in the living room. On the way to the kitchen, she paused. Pivoted. Sensed that something wasn't right yet again.

She scanned the room. Studied the sofa and love seat. The yellow pillows lining the back were still in place. The abstract metal statues propped along the glass console table hadn't been touched. Neither had the arched bronze floor lamps.

The Brazilian teak flooring creaked underneath her boots as Chloe crept across the room. She glanced down at the acrylic coffee table. The travel cocktail books were stacked neatly next to three mini succulent plants. The round silver coasters were piled inside the iron holder. The rug hadn't been shifted.

Chloe's eyes narrowed. Shifted to the table's legs. The indentations made by their feet were exposed. Someone had moved it. And it hadn't been Chloe.

Her heart bounced to the base of her throat. She grabbed her cell and turned on the flashlight. Circled the table. Searched for fingerprints, scratches or dents. Anything that would reveal an intruder had been inside her house.

A flash of light glared from the guest bedroom. Chloe's stomach dropped as she tiptoed toward the entryway and peered inside.

She ran her hand along the wall until it hit the switch. The floating ceiling light flickered on. Nothing appeared out of place. The cherrywood sleigh bed was still perfectly made. The white ergonomic chair was pushed underneath the lacquered computer desk.

"Okay, you're just seeing things…"

On the way out of the room, that flash of light flickered once again. A yellow glow poured from the closet's louvered bifold doors.

Chloe grabbed the knobs and tore the doors open. Stared up at the ceiling. The bulbs inside the flush-mount fixture shone brightly.

She hadn't turned on that light. She hadn't even been inside the closet in weeks.

"Nooo…"

Her fingers shook when she grabbed the pull string. Right before yanking it, her gaze fixated on the red silk blouse hanging in the center of the rack. It was the blouse she'd worn to the going-away party thrown by her colleagues on

her last day with the Chicago PD—the same day she went
to say goodbye to the *Chicago Force* cast and crew. And the
same day she ran into her ex Alex and his girlfriend Melissa
on her way home.

Chloe had been tempted to burn the blouse before moving back to Maxwell. Just seeing it was triggering. But she
hadn't, instead holding on to it for some reason.

One thing was for sure. Chloe had hung the blouse in the
very back of that guest-bedroom closet. Out of sight, out of
mind. That was her thought. And now, here it was. Propped
prominently in the middle with the light shining down so
that she wouldn't miss it.

Somebody had been inside her house.

Chloe charged out of the room. A shadow zoomed past
the corners of her eyes. She stopped, slowly stepping back
toward the kitchen entryway. A stream of water trickled from
the chrome high-arch spout. She hadn't left it on.

"Call Troy," Chloe breathed into her cell phone.

As it rang, she inched inside the kitchen. It was empty.
But the footsteps pounding across her backyard deck confirmed she wasn't alone.

"Hey, you," Troy said. "What's up?"

Chloe jumped at the sound of his voice booming through
the phone. Crouching down behind the island, she took a
breath. "I need you to get to my house. Immediately!"

"*Okay...* I'm actually heading that way now. What's going
on?"

"Someone's been inside my house."

"*What?* Wait—how do you know? Was a door or window
tampered with? And is anything missing?"

"No, but things are out of place," Chloe told him as she
duckwalked into the living room. Grabbing her Glock from

her purse, she headed back into the kitchen and peeked through the window.

The sound of Troy's car door slamming and engine roaring blared through the phone. "I need details, Chloe. What's out of place?"

"The coffee table and a blouse inside my closet have been moved. The water's running in the kitchen sink. And I just heard somebody running across my—"

"Hello? Chloe? You still there?"

"What the…?"

"Talk to me," Troy said. "What's happening now?"

Words turned to puffs of air as Chloe peered over the island. She stared out the window, her vision blurred with tears. There, lying in the far left corner of her backyard, was a dead body.

TROY JUMPED THE curb when he pulled up in front of Chloe's house, barely turning off the engine before hopping out and drawing his weapon. She was standing in the doorway, her right hand clutching her gun.

Without saying a word, he pointed toward the backyard. She nodded and quietly shut the front door.

Troy pressed his back against the side of the house, red bricks scraping his black bomber jacket as he crept along the driveway. He peered over the wrought iron gate. Chloe had lit the tiki lights lining the deck, illuminating the entire yard.

A sharp pain pierced his gut at the sight of the body sprawled across the lush green grass. It didn't matter that he'd already known it was there. Nothing could ever prepare him for the sight of a deceased victim.

As he made his way inside the yard, Chloe hovered in the doorway. He motioned for her to step outside. She followed his direction, and together the pair ducked down behind a wicker chaise lounge.

"Any more activity since we last spoke?" Troy whispered.

"No. Nothing. I think that shadow I saw may have been the intruder leaving out the back gate."

"Well, once we secure the area, we'll check the surveillance footage."

"I already tried while I was waiting on you to get here. The bastard uninstalled the system software that was on my computer."

"Humph. So we're not dealing with an amateur here."

"No, we are not," Chloe moaned. "I dusted the coffee table for fingerprints, too. There were none. The suspect must've been wearing gloves."

"No surprise there." Troy paused, taking in Chloe's weary expression. Her downturned lips told him everything he needed to know—she was dreading the task of analyzing the body. "You know backup is on the way. We can handle investigating the victim. You don't have to take part in that."

"Oh, no. I want to. This attack was personal. The killer wants me to be afraid. To back off of the case. And leave me in a vulnerable enough position to attack when I least expect it. The last thing I wanna do is grant him his wish. I'm not backing down from anything. Now that Dani has given me her blessing to participate in this investigation, I'm going to do everything in my power to take down the suspect."

"Good. That's exactly what I wanna hear. I think the coast is clear. Should we move in and take a closer look?"

After drawing a long breath of air, Chloe nodded. "Let's do it."

Together the pair moved toward the fence, staying low while stepping cautiously toward the back of the yard. Their heads swiveled from side to side, canvassing the area along the way.

The corner of the yard was shrouded in darkness. Just as Troy pulled out his flashlight, the faint wail of sirens whirled in the distance.

"You sure about this?" he asked. "I hear backup coming our way."

"I'm positive," Chloe whispered while looking in the other direction. "Go ahead. Turn on the flashlight. Let's see how bad it is."

Troy followed her orders, hitting the switch, then aiming the beam down at the victim.

"What in the hell…?"

"What?" Chloe breathed, her head snapping back in the direction of the body.

He tried to speak but couldn't utter a word. Chloe let off a gasp so deep that she choked.

"It's a damn mannequin!" she screeched.

"Yes, but look at what's been done to it…"

Troy guided the light along the figurine's body. The head had been removed and propped alongside the neck, which looked to have drawn-on strangulation marks. Fake blood had been splashed across its breasts, and letters were scrawled along the abdomen.

"This is so disgusting," Chloe sputtered, dropping to her knees and leaning in. "Look at the hair. It's styled just like mine. And the makeup looks like mine. This is supposed to be *me*."

Troy wanted to console her. Tell her she was wrong. Insist that the resemblance was just a coincidence. But he couldn't. Because that would've been a lie.

"Can I see that flashlight?" she asked.

He handed it over, watching as Chloe focused on the words scribbled across the stomach.

The flashlight fell from her hand. She rocked back, her head falling toward the ground.

"Are you okay?" Troy asked. She didn't respond. He knelt and wrapped an arm around her.

Pressing her body against his, she moaned, "Read what's written on it."

Troy grabbed the light and winced at the message scribbled in red paint.

YOU'RE ON MY LIST BITCH!

"I can't do this," Chloe insisted, leaping to her feet and rushing through the yard just as Maxwell PD charged through the gate.

Chapter Nine

The sight of the Kroger grocery store's parking lot sent Chloe shuddering against the driver's seat, her chest caving in disbelief. She was tempted to keep straight and head back to her house. But when an officer noticed her vehicle near the entrance, he waved her past the yellow caution tape and into the lot.

Bright light poured through the store windows as a crowd gathered near the sliding glass doors. Chloe let up on the accelerator, her tires skidding along the dark asphalt as she followed the freshly painted pavement lines. After coming to a jerking halt, she pulled into a space next to an unmarked police vehicle.

Her heart rate far exceeded its normal beat. Once she'd left Chicago behind, Chloe hadn't expected to see another crime scene again. Yet here she was, investigating not one but two cases, back to back.

Anger singed the pit of her gut as she eyed the victim's pale blue Toyota Corolla. Police tape surrounded the vehicle while law enforcement swarmed the area. A quick search for the medical examiner's van revealed the coroner had yet to arrive. An officer wearing a white hazmat suit hovered near the driver's-side door.

Leaning into the windshield, Chloe noticed the victim

slumped over the steering wheel. Her reddish-brown curls blocked her face and neck. Troy had already informed her that the woman appeared to have been strangled to death— a detail as alarming as the actual murder.

Fear trickled down Chloe's spine as she gripped her leather jacket's collar.

No time to dwell on the tragic details. There's work to be done...

She climbed out of the car and made her way toward the trunk. Waves of unease gripped her joints. But she ignored the anxiety, pulling on her protective gear and grabbing her evidence collection kit.

A long pull of air cleared a fraction of her mind as she set off toward the crime scene.

This is what you do. What you were trained to do.

The words of affirmation were reassuring. But they couldn't block out thoughts of the victim. Her lifeless body. The inevitable bruising around her neck. And the idea that Chloe was to blame for bringing a serial killer to Maxwell.

Her gait slowed as the script from *Preyed Upon*'s latest episode played in her head.

Two weeks after Sara Stewart's family reported her missing, her car was found parked in a grocery-store lot, where it had gone unnoticed for several days. Once police discovered the vehicle, they found Sara's lifeless body sitting in the driver's seat, slumped over the steering wheel. According to her autopsy report, she had been strangled to death. Sara's ex-fiancé had been considered a suspect at the time. But authorities didn't have enough evidence to prove his guilt. To this day, Sara's killer is still at large.

"Chloe!"

The soothing sound of Troy's voice pulled her back to

reality. Making his way past paramedics, he jogged over to meet her. "Thanks so much for coming out."

"Of course. I'm glad you called." Neglecting to mention her bout of angst, she pointed toward the Toyota. "Have you ID'd the victim yet?"

"We have. Her name is Jennifer Goins. The suspect left her purse sitting right on the console. So we know this wasn't a robbery."

"Any sign of sexual assault?"

"Not from what we can tell so far. She was found fully clothed in a purple hoodie and biker shorts. Of course, the medical examiner will have to confirm that. But at first glance it doesn't appear as if her clothing has been disturbed."

Chloe pulled out her cell phone and began taking notes. "Got it. Why don't we go ahead and...?" Her voice trailed off when she noticed Dani approach a group of officers, handing one of them a red biohazard bag. "You did tell Dani that you asked me to come out here, right?"

"I did. Why?"

"I'm still feeling a little uneasy after the way things went down at Jasmine's crime scene. I don't want a repeat."

"Well, there won't be. I've already reiterated how much we need you on this case. Dani actually seemed a bit pleased when I told her you were on the way."

The words were like a puppeteer, straightening Chloe's shoulders as she stood upright. "Really? That's surprising. But it's nice to hear."

"Listen, Dani's a consummate professional. You know your stuff, and as these crimes continue to escalate, I think she'll be more open to your input. Not to mention our best crime scene investigator is at the hospital."

"Oh, no. Is he okay?"

"He's fine. His wife is pregnant and went into labor this afternoon. The medical examiner is on the way, but he's driving in from Phoenix, so he won't be here for a couple of hours."

"Any good leads yet?" Chloe asked as she and Troy approached the vehicle.

"Not yet. There's no blood evidence. No shell casings. With the bruising around the victim's neck, we're guessing the cause of death is asphyxiation. But again, that'll need to be confirmed by the medical examiner. We'll send the car in for processing and see what comes back. For the time being, the team is searching for fingerprints, shoe prints, tire treads…anything that might connect us to a suspect. That could be tricky, though, considering the crime took place in a public parking lot."

Chloe removed a bottle of print-lifting graphite dust and a roll of clear adhesive tape from her kit. "Right. *If* the crime took place in the lot. The victim could've been killed at another location and brought here to throw off the investigation."

"True. I didn't even think about that. See how much we need you here?"

Nodding with thanks, she pointed toward the cameras hanging from the light poles. "What about surveillance footage? Has anybody pulled the tapes?"

"I've already spoken to the store manager, and he's gonna have the head of security email the footage to Dani. Apparently the victim's car wasn't spotted in the lot until today by a customer who noticed her collapsed over the steering wheel." Troy paused, staring up at the bright lights emanating from the poles. "Looks like the camera covering this area is pretty far off. I'm just hoping it captured something."

"That may have been done intentionally. Did you happen to see the victim's address on her ID?"

"I did. She lived over on Ember Lane. Once we're done here, I need to survey that location."

"I'd like to join you. If that's okay," Chloe quickly added.

"Of course it is."

"Hey, Detective Grant."

Dani...

Chloe almost dropped the bottle of fingerprint dust at the sound of her former title. She hadn't been called that in months.

"Hey, Chief Miller."

Addressing her ex–best friend in such a formal manner felt odd. But Chloe went with it, as she didn't want to make any missteps.

"Thanks for coming out. I'm sure Troy told you that we're short on staff. So we could really use an extra set of eyes here."

"An *experienced* extra set of eyes," he interjected.

"Yes, little brother," Dani snarked just as an officer walked over. "An experienced set of eyes."

"Chief Miller? We've got a witness here who says she may have seen something suspicious occur near the area where the victim's car is parked. She'd like to speak with you."

"Great. Tell her I'll be right there." Glancing down at the equipment in Chloe's hands, Dani asked, "Ready to search for some evidence?"

"I am. And if it's okay with you, I'd like to take a look through the victim's cell phone. Has it been retrieved?"

"It has. We found it in her purse. And I'm fine with you searching it. Now, you two get to work while I speak with this witness."

"Will do. Thanks, Dan—I mean, Chief Miller."

As the chief backed away, her lips spread into a crooked smirk—the same one she'd flash when they were kids. The sight warmed Chloe's heart. It was a reminder of how much she missed her friend.

"Looks like the officers have cleared the driver's side of the car," Troy said. "Why don't you start searching for prints while I find out which bag contains the cell?"

"Will do, thanks."

Chloe watched as Troy walked toward one of the other officers, his shoulders rolling in rhythm with each stride.

Stay focused...

She turned her attention to the vehicle, her eyes drifting from the door handle up to the victim. A piercing chill shot straight through Chloe at the sight of the dead body. No matter how many she'd seen, the visual was never easy to digest.

"Detective Grant!" Troy called out, waving a red evidence bag in the air.

She gave him a thumbs-up before sprinkling granular black powder along the door handle. Despite the urgency surrounding her, she was overcome by a sense of purpose and belonging. This was where she was supposed to be, doing exactly what she was meant to do.

It had been too long since she'd felt like a real member of a force. That feeling had disintegrated back in Chicago months before she'd actually left the department. Her squad had made sure of that. But now, even though she wasn't an official member of the Maxwell PD, that camaraderie was present. And there was no denying it felt damn good.

But the sentiment was fleeting as Chloe reminded herself of the situation at hand. She had yet to bring to Troy and Dani's attention that this murder was based on yet another episode of *Preyed Upon*.

Her phone pinged. She pulled it from her back pocket and

tapped the notification. A text appeared that had been sent from an anonymous number.

A second wave of frightening chills poured over Chloe as she stared at an attached photo. It was a close-up of the victim slumped over inside her car.

Chloe collapsed against the car when another text popped up.

Keep giving me inspiration, and I'll keep killing. Can't wait to find out whose case is up next, Cece Speaks. P.S.—You'd look great in this position…

Chapter Ten

Troy pulled his laptop closer and darkened the screen. Peering over his shoulder, he made sure Dani was nowhere near the vicinity of his cubicle. As the new chief, not only did she maintain an open-door policy to make the squad feel at ease, but she liked to walk the station floor for easier access. The efforts were good for the team. But for Troy, a pop-up wouldn't be conducive, as he was busy scrolling Chloe's Instagram feed.

He'd already set up a line of defense if Dani approached. He would tell her that he was combing through Chloe's social media accounts in search of clues. Maybe one of their suspects had liked or commented on certain posts that might appear suspicious. Someone on her followers list could stand out. There was a plethora of reasons why Troy could be observing her accounts. But while the main one was about business, there was certainly a personal interest bubbling underneath.

For now, the coast was clear. He turned back to the screen, studying each post and reading every caption. He stopped on a photo from her Chicago PD going-away party. She stood in between two officers. There were three others posing behind them. All of their faces were beaming. Troy assumed none of them were her ex-partner. He tapped the picture and checked the tags just to be sure. Detective Justin Walters's name was not listed.

Troy read the caption.

Going to miss this squad, the caption read. Lucky to have worked with some of the most amazing law enforcement officers Chicago's ever seen...

"Key word—*some*," he muttered, chuckling under his breath at Chloe's snark. While the comment might have appeared innocent to most, Troy saw straight through it. Subtle sauciness had been a trait of hers since childhood.

He thought back on the times when she and Dani would hang out at the mall during their teenage years, chasing down the newest trends while scoping out their latest crushes. The Miller parents would force Dani to take Troy along, which she couldn't stand. But he'd stay out of their way. She didn't realize he had no problem hanging in the shadows. That made it easier for him to admire Chloe from afar.

Watching her steal the show among their friends with her witty banter and snappy comebacks had been a favorite pastime. He loved observing her interactions with classmates as Chloe's warm personality and adorable giggle lit up the entire building. The most entertaining aspect of their outings would occur when she and Dani slipped into Nancy Drew mode, flexing their law enforcement prowess thanks to his father's position on the force. The girls were always on the lookout for kids trying to shoplift or workers cheating customers. They knew every mall security guard and had no qualms reporting suspicious behavior.

Chloe had always been a standout. Something about her desires felt bigger than Maxwell, even all those years ago. Troy honestly hadn't been surprised to hear she'd moved to Chicago. But he hated the fact that she had been chased out of the city thanks to a corrupt detective.

The effects of that experience were apparent. The sparkle once shining in Chloe's eyes had faded. Troy had seen a hint of it when they ran into one another at the farmers market, but it all but disappeared after the crimes being committed around Maxwell were linked back to her podcast.

He continued scrolling Chloe's Instagram feed, pausing on a Throwback Thursday post. It was an image of her and Dani, standing inside his father's office at the station. They were wearing matching pink velour tracksuits, with ponytails swinging from the tops of their heads.

This is the smile of a girl whose future was so bright, the caption read, back when I thought I'd be working for Maxwell, Arizona's police department. My childhood friend and I were in a race to see which of us would take over as police chief. Spoiler alert: She beat me to it lol...

The picture pulled at Troy's chest. It was a stark reminder of how much had changed since then—in all three of their lives. Chloe's presence had been missed, especially by Dani, who'd wanted nothing more than to work side by side with her best friend. But he'd felt her absence over the years, too. Troy might not have realized it, but even back then, he'd thought she was *the one*.

He checked the date underneath the photo. Chloe had posted it a week after she'd been attacked at the Righteous Nation's headquarters.

"Hey," Dani said, approaching from behind. "What's with the sad eyes?"

Troy slammed his laptop shut, his hand jamming in the process.

"Ow!"

"Are you okay?" she continued, moving in closer. "What are you doing?"

"Just catching up on some reports. What's up?"

She pointed at his computer, then crossed her arms over her chest. "Um, are you sure?"

"Yeah. Why?"

A twist of her lips proved she'd seen what was on his screen.

"I'm sorry," Troy continued after she failed to answer the question. "Did you say you needed something?"

The switch into sibling mode prompted a cheeky sigh to shoot from her lips. "Yeah. I was just wondering what time the meeting with you and—"

Bzzz...

Dani caught his cell phone before it vibrated off the desk. Rolling her eyes at the screen, she tossed it to him.

A text notification from Chloe was splayed across the home screen. A preview of the message was on full display.

Hey, hope your day's going well. Forgot to mention you left your baseball cap at my place. What time will you be here to pick me up?

The glare shooting from Dani's eyes singed the hairs lining Troy's forearm. He ignored the burn, responded to Chloe's text, then placed the phone back on the desk, face down this time. "Sorry about that. You were saying?"

"Just wondering what time Chloe would be here for our meeting. Clearly it'll be whatever time you pick her up, huh?"

When Troy didn't respond immediately, Dani kept going. "Have you two been hanging out?"

"We've, uh—we've just been, you know…"

Troy's voice trailed off. He couldn't bring himself to tell his sister that they'd been spending time together behind her back. But he didn't have to. His reaction said it all.

"Got it," Dani huffed, slowly backing out of the cubicle. "Well, then, I guess I'll see you two in my office whenever you bring her in."

A pang of guilt hit as Troy watched his sister walk away. He waited for her to spout off a smart remark. But she didn't. Her face had fallen, the glare in her eyes replaced by a look of hurt.

DANI STARED AT CHLOE, her inquisitive gaze intensifying by the second. The moment she and Troy had entered the chief's office, the air had thickened with tension. Glaring lights shone down from the textured white ceiling, magnifying the unease simmering between the ex-friends. The formality of it all felt surreal, as did the idea of Dani heading up an investigation that circled back to Chloe.

As Dani continued to silently stare her down, Chloe wondered if she, too, was struggling with the awkwardness. If so, she wasn't showing it. Between her squared shoulders and raised chin, Dani didn't appear the least bit fazed.

Chloe, on the other hand, sat against the back of her gray tweed chair, feeling as though she might burst into flames. When she pressed her tongue against her teeth in a desperate bid to moisten her dry mouth, Dani turned to Troy.

"Hey, Officer Miller? Would you mind grabbing Chloe a bottle of water? I think she may be a little thirsty."

The request was barely out of her mouth before he jumped out of his seat. "Of course. I'll be right back."

She still knows me inside out, Chloe thought, croaking a barely audible "Thanks."

Dani responded with a slight nod, her demeanor all business. But Chloe still knew her just as well. That weary look in her narrowing eyes said it all—the rookie chief was in over her head and appreciated Chloe's involvement in the investigation.

Once Troy closed the door behind him, a suffocating silence filled the office. Chloe didn't speak a word for fear of saying the wrong thing. Instead she glanced around the workspace, eyeing every photo and certificate hanging on the wall.

One picture in particular caught her attention. Curiosity plucked at her chest as she homed in on an image of Dani, Troy and a woman. He was standing between them, smiling for the camera while the woman stared lovingly at him.

The twinge of inquisitiveness deepened when Chloe realized she'd seen her before. Troy had posted pictures of them together on his social media accounts. Chloe was under the impression they'd broken up. But if that were true, why would Dani still have a photo of them hanging on the wall?

"So," Dani said, slamming a notebook onto her desk and flipping it open, "this podcast of yours, *Preyed Upon*. We've talked a little bit about it. But tell me more."

Anxiety grabbed hold of Chloe's throat as she peered across the desk at her ex–best friend. The moment felt surreal, more like a warped vision than an actual moment in time.

"Sorry about that," Troy said, strolling back into the office with three bottles of water in hand. He closed the door behind him and handed one to Chloe before taking a seat next to her. "Officer Keller caught me in the hallway, asking for a quick debriefing on the case. What'd I miss?"

Chloe's gaze went straight to the photo of him and the woman as Dani replied, "Not much. We were just getting into the concept behind *Preyed Upon*."

Both she and Troy turned to Chloe, who cracked open her water and took several long gulps.

"Well…" she rasped, clearing her airway before continuing, "I launched the podcast soon after moving back to Maxwell. I was just looking for some sort of outlet after I retired from the Chicago PD. It was my way of staying close to the true crime community and keeping my mind occupied after everything that went down before I retired."

"And these cases you've been discussing," Dani continued. "They're similar to the crimes that have been committed here in Maxwell?"

"No, not similar. They're exact copycats of the cases I've discussed."

As Chloe eyed the bullet points Dani scribbled in her notebook, Troy gave her a nudge, mouthing the words *you're doing great.*

"Thanks," she whispered, the tension in her shoulders easing up a bit.

"So you're telling me that Jasmine Bailey," Dani said, "who was stabbed to death in front of her house, was killed in a manner similar to a case you covered on your podcast?"

"Again, not similar. Exact. Those two murders matched up to a T. Down to the bite mark on Jasmine's left cheek."

"So you don't think this is all just a coincidence? You're *convinced* that someone's trying to taunt you?"

"At this point, I'm one hundred percent sure that someone's trying to taunt me."

Dani bit down on her thumbnail, tapping her pen against the edge of the desk. "Any idea why the killer would've chosen Jasmine?"

Raising a finger in the air, Troy asked, "Is it all right if I take this one?"

Both he and Chloe looked to Dani for permission. She rocked back in her chair, waving her hand before replying, "Go on. I'm listening."

"When Chloe first moved back to Maxwell, she ran into Jasmine at the farmers market. They had a conversation out in the open. Maybe the killer was watching Chloe, saw them talking and targeted Jasmine after realizing they know one another. He did mention the Nike trainers Jasmine was wearing that day in the note he left with the dead flower stems."

"Which, in a roundabout way, would've made it a personal attack against Chloe?"

"Yes. Exactly."

The chief's eyelids fluttered as she picked up her pen. "Okay, now this is starting to make a little more sense. But here's what doesn't. Chloe, Troy mentioned that *Preyed Upon* is hosted anonymously and that you use an alias. If these are all personal attacks against you, how would anyone know that you're the person behind the mic?"

"We're thinking that someone may have recognized my voice."

Dani's note-taking came to an abrupt halt. "Wait—you record the podcast using your own voice instead of speech-altering software?"

"I do. I tried that method, but it felt so inauthentic. Some of my words were unclear and distorted. And using a fake voice made me feel as if I wasn't doing these victims justice. It just didn't seem as impactful as my own voice."

"So that was more important to you than your personal safety?"

"I— Well…of course not," Chloe stuttered, her cheeks tingling with embarrassment. "I guess I didn't think things all the way through. I was just focused on getting started, then keeping the momentum going once my mood improved and the number of listeners increased. There are millions of podcasts out there. I never would've thought someone I know would pick up on mine and know it's me."

"I'd have to agree with you on the *you didn't think* part," Dani muttered under her breath. "But I get it," she added, her expression softening. "You've been through a lot. So I can understand the podcast being therapeutic."

The surprising response was comforting, reminding Chloe of who Dani once was. A confidante. An advocate. That reassuring friend who always found a way to put her at ease.

"You're right," Chloe told her. "*Preyed Upon* has definitely been therapeutic. Honestly, it saved me. My work in criminal justice meant everything to me. To have it snatched away was traumatizing. In a way, I felt victimized. So telling these stories and bringing awareness to listeners has been rewarding. Which is what makes everything that's happening here in Maxwell all the more painful."

Troy reached over and clutched her hand. The move sent Dani's tight gaze shooting toward their grip. Expecting a brusque response, Chloe braced herself, her toes tightening inside her fringed suede booties.

"I can imagine you being traumatized," Dani said. "Just trust that the department will be putting all of its resources behind solving this case. Now, getting back to the podcast and someone figuring out it's you. You're saying that our suspect may have recognized your voice, or…"

"Or maybe traced an email address back to Chloe," Troy interjected. "She could've even slipped up and accidentally revealed a small detail about her life that somebody who knows her picked up on. There are several factors that could have done it."

Swiveling in her chair, Dani pressed her fingertips together while eyeing the ceiling. "So now that the cat's out the bag, we need to identify a person or persons of interest. Have you thought about who'd do something like this? And why?"

"We have, actually. Troy and I put together a list of possible suspects and the reasons we think they're targeting me. Starting with Jasmine's ex-boyfriend Darren Simmons."

"You can cross him off the list."

"Really? Why?"

"I brought him in for questioning this morning. He has a solid alibi."

"Why am I just now hearing about this?" Troy asked.

"He arrived before you got to the station. We haven't had a chance to talk, since you've clearly been busy…"

Troy responded with a grunt and released Chloe's hand.

"So what was Darren's story?" Troy continued.

"He'd gotten home from work a little after seven in the evening. Didn't leave the house again until a quarter to six the next morning. His wife backed him up on that, too. According to the medical examiner, Jasmine's death most likely occurred between the hours of nine and ten that night."

"What about surveillance footage from Darren's house? Or a neighbor's house proving his entry and exit times?"

"According to Darren, it's all stored on his computer. He's gonna email the footage to me."

"And his phone records?" Troy pressed. "Are you planning on looking into his call log and text messages?"

"Absolutely. We'll have his provider pull the cell tower location history, too. No stone will be left unturned."

Chloe ran her hands down the sides of her face in frustration. "Well, I won't pass judgment until I have all the facts. But if I'm being honest, I don't think Darren is our guy."

"What about the way he reacted when we questioned him at Jasmine's funeral?" Troy probed. "All the fidgeting and sweating. Not to mention the stammering."

"I think that was about the guilt he feels for the way he treated Jasmine back in the day. And knowing that we're all aware of his behavior. When it comes to her murder, however, my gut is telling me that he's not involved."

"You know, at this point, so is mine," Troy stated. "But we'll know for sure once we review the surveillance footage and cell phone records."

A knock on the desk turned their attention back to Dani, whose head was swiveling back and forth between the pair. "You two seem to have grown pretty close since you returned to Maxwell, Chloe."

Her exaggerated tone was seasoned with sarcasm. The room fell silent despite Dani's expectant pause. She'd always been a possessive friend, even as a young child. While their ties had severed years ago, Chloe wasn't surprised by the resentment toward her and Troy's connection.

"Yeah," he replied. "It's been nice…linking up with old acquaintances. Especially after Chloe and I both spent so much time away from Maxwell. There's a lot that we can relate to."

The twitch of Dani's nose revealed what words didn't— she sensed the burgeoning feelings brewing between the pair.

"Once you take a look at the list of suspects," Troy continued, sliding it across the desk, "you'll see that there are several people we believe could be behind this. There's an overzealous superfan of the podcast named Gretchen, who's made several attempts to identify and befriend Chloe. An ex-boyfriend who'd given Chloe some trouble after the breakup—"

"Wait," Dani interjected. "It isn't Alex, is it?"

"I… It is," Chloe barely managed to confirm, considering the relationship was such a point of contention between her and Dani. "We added his current girlfriend to the list as well since she had issues with me, too. Her name is Melissa Chaney."

Chloe picked at a chip in her nude nail polish, sensing Dani's urge to shoot back *I told you so* or *you should've listened to me*.

But instead, the chief said, "Duly noted. And I see there

are more names on this list. A writer on *The Chicago Force*, several members of the Chicago PD… Troy told me about what occurred during that final sting operation. The one that sent you into retirement. I'm sorry you went through that."

The statement lifted Chloe's head. Her body warmed with relief at Dani's soft smile. It was a look of empathy. And compassion. One that Chloe had thought her former friend would never offer up again.

"The thought of you being put in such danger by fellow officers is disturbing, to say the least," Dani asserted. "Especially after being surrounded by law enforcement all your life. We always understood their duty to serve society. Not themselves. But I get that everyone isn't like us." She hesitated, turning her head while blinking rapidly. "That's why I wish you would've just stayed…"

Her head dipped as her voice faded. She grabbed the list and continued reading rather than finishing her statement. But there was no need. Chloe knew how it would've ended.

That's why I wish you would've just stayed here in Maxwell.

The room fell silent once again. Chloe peered over at Troy, her bottom lip tightening.

I don't know what to say! her wide eyes screamed. With a spin of her hand down by her side, she gestured for Troy to speak up.

"So, um…" he began, sliding to the edge of his chair, "now that you've got a list of names, where should we go from here?"

"For starters, I'd like to do a deep dive on these people. Check out their social media accounts. See if we can figure out their whereabouts around the time that the murders took place. Find out who may have been away from their jobs. Print out their photos and pass them around the station so that officers can keep an eye out in case one of them pops up around town. Maxwell PD's presence will be heavy all over town, and the community will be put on high alert. In the meantime, Chloe, you need to stay vigilant. Keep your eyes open and your weapon close by at all times. Assuming you're still in possession of a weapon?"

"Of course. These days I don't leave home without it."

"Good. Let's keep it that way. I'd like to put your house under surveillance, too, since we know the suspect's been in Maxwell and may have followed you home at some point. Are you okay with that?"

Chloe's head tilted in surprise. "Yes, most definitely. Thank you."

Their falling-out had left Chloe fearing that Dani wouldn't take the attacks against her seriously. Or that she'd doubt the validity of them being personal. Her show of concern was reassuring, giving Chloe the sense of security she'd been craving—the security that had eluded her back in Chicago.

She thought back on the decision to leave Maxwell behind for a man who didn't deserve her. And breaking the promise she'd made all those years ago to work side by side with Dani, the one person who'd always had her back. Chicago had left her with some good memories. But they were far outweighed by the bad. Colleagues turning on her, the man she loved betraying her trust, a writer wanting to harm her over lines in a script…

Regret pounded her head as she sat across from Dani, feeling small and defeated. While Chloe had been over fifteen hundred miles away, tumbling through a 360-degree circle of deceit, Dani was working toward becoming their hometown's police chief. And now here she was, goal accomplished, while Chloe was right back where she'd started, with nothing to show for all those years she'd been gone.

You messed up. Bad...

"So why don't I do this?" Dani said while jotting notes. "I'll check in with my officers and see who's available to take on the surveillance shifts throughout the day."

"I've got a suggestion," Troy interjected. "Since you've already got a lot on your plate, I'd be happy to help schedule those shifts."

"Aw, Officer Miller, that's awfully kind of you," Dani gushed through a bemused side-eye. "Thanks so much for thinking of me. Sure, be my guest. Just make sure you get started on it as soon as possible. I'd like to get eyes on Chloe's house today."

"Will do. And if I have trouble finding someone to cover, I'm available. I mean, you know. Since it's pretty short notice and all."

"I bet you are..."

"Chief Miller, could you please stop with the—"

She slammed her notebook shut, cutting Troy off midsentence. "In the meantime, we'll start looking into these suspects. I'll have my digital forensic investigator, Chuck, do some digging on this Gretchen Knight. See if she's involved in some way. I'll also have him look deeper into those weird text messages you've been getting." She paused when her cell phone buzzed against the keyboard. "Okay, I need to get to my city council meeting. Chloe, thanks again for coming down and providing us with this information. It's very helpful. And, uh...it was good seeing you again."

"You, too, Dani," she echoed, almost feeling as though she were floating when she stood. "There's one more thing I'd like to mention, if that's okay."

"Sure. Walk with me while I head to the ladies' room."

The women walked side by side down the hallway while Troy trailed them.

"So…listen," Chloe began. "I know I'm not a member of the Maxwell PD. But I gained a ton of experience investigating murders back in Chicago. When it comes to this case, you were gracious enough to give me access to Jasmine's crime scene as well as Jennifer's. If it isn't too much to ask, I'd love to get more involved. Maybe on a consultant-type basis."

She paused, waiting for some sort of reaction. But Dani remained stone-faced.

You've overstepped your bounds…

Determination encouraged her to press on.

"That is, if I wouldn't be too much of an imposition."

Stopping abruptly in the middle of the hallway, Dani stared down at the white speckled tile. Several moments passed before she finally replied, "Sure. I think that would be good for the department."

Chloe swallowed the ball of emotion creeping up her throat. While it was the response she wanted, it wasn't the one she'd expected.

"Great. Thank you so much. I look forward to getting started."

"Same here. Listen, I need to get going. We'll talk soon. In the meantime, Officer Miller, can you make sure Chloe gets home safely?"

"Absolutely, Chief."

The soles of Chloe's feet tingled as the pair made their way to the parking lot. It was a sensation she'd experienced every time a new investigation was underway. Her mind was already churning in a thousand directions on how to approach the case.

Being back in law enforcement in an official capacity felt invigorating, despite the dire circumstances surrounding them. So did reconnecting with Dani, even though it was in a business capacity.

As Troy opened the car door for her, Chloe contemplated what was just as prevalent in the investigation—the opportunity to work closely with him.

Chapter Eleven

Troy and Chloe had been holed up inside his apartment for hours building a criminal profile. Ever since Darren's alibi checked out, she'd been working the case nonstop, determined to nail down a suspect. Troy had suggested they take a food break at least three times. But she wasn't ready to stop. Not until they were done.

He knew that wasn't the only reason Chloe had buried herself in the assignment. After their second victim turned up dead, she'd put her podcast on an indefinite hold.

"Maybe if I stop reporting on these murders," she'd said, "the killings will stop. No *Preyed Upon*, no inspiration to copy the crimes."

"Let's hope so," Troy had told her.

While Chloe knew it was the right thing to do, Troy could tell the void was getting to her—to the point where she'd dived even deeper into investigation in an effort to fill it.

"Whew," he sighed, tossing his pen onto the round oak dining table and pressing his palms against his eyes. He'd been staring at the computer screen for so long that his vision had blurred. His right wrist ached from all the note-taking. But Chloe was still at it, her tortoise-framed blue-light glasses slipping down the bridge of her nose as she banged away on the keyboard.

Stretching against the back of his chair, he shifted his pupils from right to left, focusing on various objects in his short-term one-bedroom apartment. Troy had no excuse as to why he was still living there. He'd moved back to Maxwell so quickly after Dani had been named chief of police that he hadn't had time to find a permanent place. There was no way he would've moved back in with their parents. And he'd refused to live with his sister. The siblings' relationship was great, and he wanted to keep it that way. While Troy was laid-back, Dani was uptight, especially when it came to her personal space. He went to bed early, while she was a night owl. He enjoyed his solitude, and she loved to entertain. Co-habitating never would've worked. So he'd settled on temporary housing and had been there ever since.

What should've been an eight-week situation had lasted for months. Troy was so busy focusing on reacclimating himself to Maxwell and adjusting to the new job that he'd neglected to find a permanent home. So while the apartment's neutral, minimalist decor was fairly modest, and two people could barely fit in the galley kitchen at once, he'd managed to make do.

A thunderous rumble surged through his stomach like the first wave of a tsunami. Troy looked over at Chloe, certain that she'd heard it. But her eyes were still glued to her laptop.

That's it...

He grabbed his cell and pulled up the Quick Eats app.

"So, what do you have a taste for?" he asked, scrolling through the list of restaurants. The approach was more aggressive than the last. It was no longer a question of whether or not she was ready to eat. It was more of a *we're going to eat, so what do you want?* sort of thing.

"Give me one sec," she muttered without looking up from the screen.

"I'm thinking either pizza or ramen. Which would you like?"

Silence.

"Speak now or forever hold your peace."

Chloe held up a finger without saying a word.

"All right, then. Pizza it is."

Just as Troy tapped the Sliced to Perfection menu, his intercom buzzed.

"What was that?" Chloe breathed, lurching in her chair.

"It's just the intercom. But I don't know who it could be. I'm not expecting anybody."

As he stood, Troy noticed her head swivel toward the door, deep wrinkles creasing her forehead.

"What's wrong?" he asked.

"I don't know. Probably just my PTSD acting up…"

"Well, if it's any consolation, just know that I'm not gonna let anything happen to you. Not to mention you're a highly trained law enforcement officer, and we're both armed… I highly doubt that anybody would have the nerve to come here and try either of us."

His words didn't seem to move her as she remained in the same stiff position, her eyes still glued to the door.

Pressing the talk button, he barked, "Who is it?" and hoped the gruff tone would put Chloe at ease.

"It's your sister. Why are you answering the door sounding like Mr. T?"

"Because I had no clue you were stopping by. And there's some crazed killer running around Maxwell stalking Chloe, who, as you know, is here with me. But anyway, come on up."

Troy opened the door before Dani could knock. When he saw her carrying a bag from the Burger Haven, he almost scooped her up and twirled her around the room.

"Please tell me there's enough food in that bag for three."

"There's probably enough food in this bag for six."

"My prayers have been answered…"

"Here," Dani said, handing it to him. "Why don't you plate everything while I have a talk with Chloe? If that's all right with you."

"Of course it is. Why wouldn't it be?"

She moved in close and whispered, "I haven't been the nicest since she's moved back. Chloe's going through a lot and could use my support. Plus, if she's gonna be helping with the investigation, I need to make peace with her."

"I like that idea," Troy responded with a smile. "You go talk to her while I head to the kitchen."

He watched as Dani timidly stepped to the table. It was a rare sighting, seeing his sister take on such a humble approach. Humility looked good on her. While there wasn't much that warmed his heart, it felt good seeing Dani put the past behind her and reconcile with the best friend she'd ever had.

"Hey," Troy heard Dani say. "Mind if I join you?"

"Not at all. Please, have a seat."

"Thanks. I hope you're hungry, because I brought food. *A lot* of food. From the Burger Haven."

"Oh, really? So you remembered, huh."

"Absolutely. How could I forget one of your favorite places to eat? I knew your order, too. One broiled chicken sandwich with cheddar cheese and bacon, a small order of onion rings, and a side of homemade potato chips."

"You got it. Thank you. So, um…what's the occasion?"

Troy picked up on the surprise in Chloe's high-pitched tone. He quieted the rattling plates hitting the countertop so as not to miss a word of the conversation.

"Consider it an olive branch of sorts. My way of apologizing for being so cold when you first moved back. And everything that went down between us in the past. I know I didn't handle myself well when you left. That was pretty immature of me. But I had such high hopes of us living out our dreams together here in Maxwell. So when you skipped town, it crushed me. Then we lost touch, and that *really* did me in."

"I'm so sorry," Chloe whispered, her trembling voice barely audible.

"And don't get me wrong. I think it's great that you stuck to your goals and pursued your career in Chicago. But you have to admit, your relationship with Alex had a negative effect on our friendship. Remember how he insisted that I was too dependent on you?"

"I do remember that."

"What he didn't know is that our friendship was built on support. And back then, I really could've used yours. There were times when I didn't think I'd make it out of the police academy. That training was so tough. Imagine how embarrassing it would've been for my family had I not graduated. I always thought things would have been easier if you were there with me. But you weren't. So the next best thing would've been moral support, even if it was long-distance."

"And I should've given you that. I should not have let Alex get inside my head to the point where I wasn't there for you. Again, I'm sorry. I should have been a better friend, period."

"I accept your apology. I'm just glad we've both matured, grown from that situation and moved on."

Leaping from her chair, Chloe threw her arms around Dani as squeals of elation filled the room. "I'm so happy to hear you say that. Looking back, I wish I'd been more transparent before moving away. But I was so afraid of telling you, especially because I knew how you felt about Alex. You were right about him, too, obviously. He wasn't the one, and I should've listened to—"

"No," Dani interrupted. "You should've done exactly what

you did. Relocated to Chicago and lived your life. Dreams change. You followed your heart. There's nothing wrong with that. You came back home with some great memories. Memories that I'll never get to experience because I chose to play it safe. Stay here in Maxwell. Where has that gotten me?"

"Um, to chief-of-police status."

"Yeah, but I'm still single, and—"

"So am I," Chloe interrupted.

"But at least you can say you had a fiancé at one point."

"Technically, Alex and I were never really engaged."

"Well, at least the topic of marriage was on the table," Dani argued. "All I've had is a string of half-assed relationships with men who I judged based on their potential rather than their reality."

Okay, that's enough, Troy thought, growing irritated with talk of Chloe's past relationship. He grabbed the food and made his way back into the dining room. "Who's ready to eat?"

"I am!" Chloe declared, snatching her plate and digging in before he'd even sat down.

"Oh, *really*?" Troy replied with a chuckle. "Not you. You couldn't possibly be hungry after the way you ignored every one of my requests to order lunch."

"That was before my favorite Burger Haven meal arrived."

Dani glanced over at Troy's notebook. "Hey, what's with the extensive bullet list?"

"That's the criminal profile we've been working on all day. Do you want to hear what we've got?"

"Yes, definitely. And when you're done with that, I have some information to share with you both. I didn't just come here bearing food and apologies. But you first. Let's hear the details on this profile."

"So we're thinking that the suspect is male and between the ages of thirty-five and forty-five."

"Okay, so not a young buck, then."

"Definitely not," Chloe chimed in between bites of chips. "This guy has some life experience under his belt. And when it comes to the law? We believe he possesses a good amount of knowledge."

Dani tapped her fingernails against the table while staring out a small casement window. "Well, judging by the list of suspects you two already gave me, it could be your ex-partner Justin. Or your ex-boyfriend Alex. His girlfriend-slash-paralegal, Melissa, might very well be in on it, too."

"And the head writer on *The Chicago Force*, Simon. Don't forget about him. He knows his way around the law thanks to all the police procedural research he does for the show. Even though it oftentimes wasn't accurate."

"Duly noted," Dani said. "So go on. Tell me some of the other traits of the suspect."

"We think he's highly intelligent," Troy responded, "and methodical. From the victims he's choosing to the way he's killing them, his plan is well-thought-out. Almost to the point of obsession. Which is directly tied to the way he's copied the *Preyed Upon* episodes to a T."

"We also believe he's a depraved thrill seeker," Chloe added. "These are big crimes being committed that'll draw a lot of attention. The suspect isn't sexually motivated, which makes sense. None of the victims I've discussed on the podcast were sexually assaulted. What's interesting is that these traits could eliminate our other suspect, Gretchen Knight, better known as *Preyed Upon*'s superfan. But everything I know about her is based on an online persona. In reality, she could be a male who fits our profile."

"Gretchen Knight," Dani repeated, reaching into her leather tote and pulling out a file folder. "She's actually one of the reasons why I'm here. Our digital forensic investigator did some pretty extensive digging. He was able to pull an IP address from her *Preyed Upon* subscription. It was traced back to a college student in Sydney, Australia. Gretchen Knight is her real name, so she's not going by a pseudonym. We contacted the New South Wales police department, who reached out to Macquarie University's dean of students. They confirmed that Gretchen was on the other side of the world when the murders took place."

"All right," Chloe said, crossing out her name. "And then there were four."

"That's not all I've got," Dani said.

"Oh, there's more?"

"Yep. I finally heard back from the manager at Kroger. That surveillance footage we'd been waiting on? It didn't reveal anything that happened to the victim."

Troy's arms flew out at his sides. "How is that even possible? Jennifer's car was literally parked right underneath a surveillance camera!"

"Here's how."

Dani pulled out her laptop, opened an email and clicked on a video. Kroger's parking lot came into view. The recording was time-stamped 2:43 a.m., and the date matched up with the day Jennifer's body was found. The lot was empty, as the store had closed at 11:00 p.m.

The black-and-white footage was haunting, like a scene straight out of Alfred Hitchcock's *Psycho*. Subdued lights shone against the dull asphalt. Shadows loomed in the background. An eerie stillness lingered in the air, as if they were looking at a photo rather than a video.

"Is anything going to happen here?" Chloe asked.

"Just keep watching."

More than two minutes passed before a figure entered the frame. He appeared to be male, tall and solidly built. A baseball cap, balaclava and dark clothing disguised his identity. No vehicle came into view, as he was on foot.

The man walked to the perimeter of the area where the victim's car had been found.

"Look at him," Troy said. "Scoping out the scene before committing the crime."

"It's sickening," Dani added with a shudder, "knowing what's gonna happen within twenty-four hours of this footage being recorded."

The man paced the parking space where the victim's car had been found, then approached a nearby light pole. His head tilted toward the top of it, his face staring directly at the camera. While the light shone down on him, nothing identifiable appeared through the black cap and ski mask.

Several moments passed before he took a step back. Spun a 360, as if to see whether anyone was watching. He dug around inside his field-jacket pocket and pulled something out. It flashed underneath the light's beam.

"Is that a gun?" Chloe asked.

Before Dani could respond, the man took aim and fired at the camera.

"Damn!" Chloe gasped.

"Everywhere we turn," Troy rasped after the video went black, "we're getting blocked. This guy is staying ten steps ahead of us. Was that the only camera recording the space where Jennifer's body was found?"

"Yes, unfortunately," Dani confirmed. "I viewed the footage from the other cameras and came up empty."

Knocking her fist against the edge of the table, Chloe said, "This maniac knows what he's doing. And he is leaving no stone unturned. Like we said in our criminal profile, he's a meticulous, thrill-seeking predator."

"In other words, your typical serial killer." Dani slammed her laptop shut. "Oh, well. Back to the drawing board. But in the meantime, let's eat."

Chapter Twelve

Chloe pulled out of the Best Buy parking lot and pressed the accelerator, eager to get home. The day had been long. And grueling. After the Maxwell PD's murder investigation stalled, Chloe grew antsy. She'd needed something to take her mind off of the case. So she decided to record an episode of *Preyed Upon* and shelve it until the podcast was back up and running.

After reading through her notes, Chloe realized she never did record Brooklyn Williams's episode, the college student whose roommate killed her with a tennis racket. Reporting on the case had been emotionally draining. Detailing the decline of the friendship. The brutality behind Brooklyn's murder. Her roommate Tanya's subsequent life sentence. Two lives ruined. Two families left in pain as they suffered the consequences of one woman's actions.

While recording, Chloe couldn't help but think of her and Dani's broken friendship. Of course, they'd never gotten close to a physical altercation. But Brooklyn and Tanya's volatile relationship and violent ending left Chloe grateful that she and Dani had managed to reconcile after their complicated falling-out.

By the time she'd finished editing the episode, Chloe was feeling so overwhelmed that she'd torn her headphones off too quickly, ripping one of the ear-pad cushions. She had spent more time being annoyed about it than it took to replace them. And now, as she headed home from picking up a new pair, Chloe put all thoughts of *Preyed Upon* out of her mind and focused on seeing Troy later that evening.

While she hated to admit it, he had her spoiled. Troy was the only person she'd been communicating with on a daily basis. She was slowly growing dependent on his companionship—to the point where she certainly couldn't deny her burgeoning feelings.

But it wasn't her fault. Troy knew what he was doing, pouring on the charm while seducing her in the most innocent of ways. The way his eyes crinkled in the corners when he flashed a sexy half smile. And when he'd touch her thigh or squeeze her arm whenever she cracked a joke. Or how he'd look for reasons to call or get together.

Never in her wildest dreams had Chloe seen herself dating a younger man—especially Troy, also known as Dani's annoying little brother for most of her life. The one who'd hide their makeup, change the channel while they watched their favorite shows and prank call Chloe's house, acting as if he were a secret admirer. She realized he'd probably been crushing on her for years. Little did she know those feelings would one day be mutual.

A red light pulled Chloe from her thoughts. She slammed on the brakes before she veered into the intersection. The car behind her blared its horn after almost ramming her bumper.

"Sorry!" she yelled into the rearview mirror, as if the driver could hear her. She gave him an apologetic wave. He didn't acknowledge the gesture.

"Jerk," she muttered, staring at the man through the side-view mirror. Between the darkness of the night and the black

hoodie covering the majority of his face, Chloe couldn't get a good look at him.

Beeep!

Her head popped up toward the traffic light. It had turned green.

The driver behind her laid on his horn.

"All right, I'm going! What is your *problem*...?"

Acacia Avenue came into view. Chloe clicked her right turn signal, glad to get away from the agitated tailgater.

Thoughts of Troy coming to her place later that night put her mind at ease. It was their official makeup date after he'd missed the hike along the Sandstone Peak Mountain Preserve. Since he and Chloe were both exhausted, they'd tossed around the idea of ordering in. He suggested burrito bowls or spicy noodles. But Chloe suddenly felt a second wind coming on. A nice home-cooked meal would be way more satisfying. Maybe a couple of grilled rib-eye steaks or pan-seared lamb chops.

A roundup of her refrigerator's contents rolled through her head. Just as she contemplated stopping by the grocery store, a pair of high beams flickered behind her.

"What are you *doing*?" Chloe barked toward the mirror.

The tailgater was at it again. Thankfully she'd reached the intersection with Acacia Avenue.

Chloe eased up on the accelerator ever so slightly, her tires screeching as she sped around the corner. A puff of relief shot through her lips. But one glance in the rearview mirror and she saw that the driver had made the turn, too.

"You have *got* to be kidding me..."

She considered pulling over and letting him pass. But Chloe didn't want to stop. There was no telling who was behind the wheel and what they might do.

Call Troy, she thought before quickly changing her mind.

Chloe didn't want to appear paranoid. The driver hadn't done anything to harm her. Plus, having a bad attitude wasn't against the law.

She sped up a bit. The car behind followed suit. She switched lanes and slowed down, hoping he'd pass her by. Instead he switched lanes as well, his front plate now inches from her bumper.

"Oh, so you wanna play games, huh," Chloe muttered, her eyes darting back and forth between the rearview mirror and the road. "Okay. I've got something for you…"

She glanced over at the passenger seat, eyeing her tote bag.

Get it, she told herself before pulling her gun from the side pocket and placing it on her lap.

Adjusting the side-view mirror, she noticed the car had slowed down. The distance eased the heaving in her chest. Nevertheless, she contemplated making a U-turn and heading to the police station.

Her hands tightened around the steering wheel as she focused on the road. The surrounding darkness swallowed her up like an endless tunnel. Acacia was a fairly desolate street. There were very few cars in the vicinity. The ones that she could make out were a significant distance away. But the car behind her was still close and inching closer.

Rockwood Drive appeared up ahead. A left would take Chloe straight home. But there was no way in hell she'd hook the turn with the tailgater riding her bumper.

She gripped the wheel with one hand while clutching her Glock with the other. Although she was armed, Chloe couldn't ease the dread coursing through her body. Reality flashed before her, glaring brighter than the driver's lights beaming from behind. Had the person sending those bizarre text messages finally caught up to her?

Vrooom!

She jolted in her seat as the driver sped up. He was so close that Chloe could no longer make out the front end of his vehicle. She floored the accelerator. But it didn't matter. His relentless pursuit wouldn't let up.

Pounding the steering wheel's push-to-talk button, Chloe yelled, "Call Troy!"

He picked up on the first ring. "Hey, what's up? I was just getting ready to call you—"

"Hold on, Troy. Somebody's following me!" The words tumbled out of her mouth in a tangled flurry.

"Slow down, Chloe. I can't understand you. What's going on?"

"I'm being followed!"

"Where are you?"

"Acacia Avenue. I was on my way home from Best Buy, and some crazed maniac has been tailgating me ever since. Of course, I can't go to my house now. I'm approaching Indigo Lane. Should I take that to the police station?"

"*Yes.* And while you're heading this way, I'll jump in the car and meet up with you. Maybe we can catch this bastard and block him in."

"Yeah, that's if he doesn't crash into me before I get there."

"Try your best to outmaneuver him. Do you have your weapon on you?"

"Right in my hand. And I'm prepared to shoot if necessary."

Chloe made the turn onto Indigo. The driver followed, jumping the curb while continuing to tail her. His engine growled so violently that it rattled her car's interior.

"Do you hear that?" she screeched.

"I do. Listen, don't let him intimidate you. Put those high-level driving skills of yours to good use. I'm on my way. And I've got backup coming, too."

Hearing that eased the rumble of panic banging inside her chest. "Thank you, Troy. I really appreciate you."

"You don't have to thank me. I'm just doing my job."

She knew there was more to it than that. But whether business or personal, she was beyond grateful for him. For more than just his protection.

Boom!

"Aaah!" Chloe screamed after her head hit the window.

The steering wheel jerked from side to side as she skidded along the shoulder, barely avoiding the guardrail.

"Chloe! What's going on?"

"This guy just hit me!"

"Okay. Hang on. I'm trying to get to you as fast as I can."

Once she regained control of the car, Chloe clutched her throbbing forehead and peered through the rearview mirror. Haze blocked her vision. The road appeared smoky, as if a fog machine had unleashed liquid nitrogen across the asphalt.

"Talk to me, Chloe. Are you okay?"

"I am," she sniffed as sirens wailed in the distance. "Is that your car I hear?"

"It is. Flash your headlights so I'll know where you are."

She followed his command while praying the attacker wouldn't strike again. "Can you see me?"

"I can. And I see the vehicle trailing you, too. Listen, slow down. I'm gonna turn off my siren so the driver won't know I'm on the way. Once you drive past me, I'll hook a quick U-turn and follow behind him. You stop, and we'll pin him in. Got it?"

"Got it."

Sucking in a breath of air, Chloe watched as Troy's sedan loomed closer. Her calf muscles tensed as she let up on the accelerator.

"I'm ready," she uttered, preparing to come to a full stop once he was in position.

His car spun around. Just as he fell in line, the attacker turned off his headlights and swerved onto a remote road.

"Damn it!" Chloe shrieked before realizing exactly where he'd veered off. "Oh, wait. He won't get very far. That isn't even an actual street. It leads to a dead end."

"No, it doesn't. Not anymore, at least. The Department of Transportation opened it up last year. It's a through street now. Kent Trail. Turn around and follow me!"

The bitter stench of burning rubber filled Chloe's car. She made a sharp U-turn and trailed Troy's vehicle. Leaning against the door, she peered past his sedan and into the darkness. "Wait—where did he go? I don't see anybody in front of you!"

"Yeah…" Troy muttered, his gravelly voice oozing defeat. "Neither do I. But let's keep going and try to catch up with him. In the meantime, I'll hit the radio. Let backup know to look for a small black sports car with front-end damage. I tried to make out the license plate but couldn't. It's too dark."

"Neither could I."

The pair fell silent as Chloe continued to follow Troy. They zoomed past several Maxwell PD vehicles, all on the hunt for the rogue driver. Thirty minutes passed with no luck. Chloe was growing weary. And hopeless. And even more fearful.

"Hey," Troy murmured, "you're awfully quiet. Are you okay?"

"Not really. But I will be. Eventually." Even she could hear the lack of conviction in her flat tone.

"I'll tell you what. Why don't I have Dani tell the team to keep searching for this guy while we head back to your place? I think you need to decompress. We can get back to it tomorrow. What do you think?"

"I think that's a good idea. I'm right behind you."

Chapter Thirteen

Troy followed Chloe into her house, fighting the urge to pull her down onto the couch. Hold her in his arms. And vow to never leave her side again.

He struggled to fight off thoughts of the assailant harming her. Guilt rattled his mind like a caged animal. Troy knew the chase wasn't his fault. But he couldn't help but blame himself.

"Stop it," she whispered, grasping his hand as they stood in the middle of the living room.

"Stop what?"

"Carrying the burden of what happened tonight on your shoulders."

"And how do you know that's what I'm doing?"

"It's written in between those lines of frustration surrounding that frown," Chloe said, running her soft fingertips along his skin. "And I can see it in your weary eyes. There's nothing you could've done to prevent it."

Troy's jaws tightened as he went into defense mode. But before he could say another word, she whispered, "It's okay. Just let it go."

Her soft expression disarmed him. "You shouldn't be consoling me right now. I should be comforting you."

"Listen. Tonight was a lot. There's no denying that. But

I'm strong. This isn't my first rodeo and it probably won't be my last. I may be a little shaken up, but I got through it. Things could've been worse. For now, it's over. So let's just focus on figuring out who's behind all this. The chase, the texts, the murders."

"You got it." Troy studied her face, running his finger along the slight bump on her forehead. "Did this happen when he hit your car?"

"It did."

"Should I take you to the hospital so you can get it checked out?"

"No. I'm fine. It's nothing a little ice and pain medication won't fix."

"Well, if you change your mind, just let me know."

Seeing Chloe hurt pained him. Frazzled, he motioned toward the couch. "Why don't we take a load off? Sit down and start working on a police report so we can…" His voice faded when she blew a low moan. "Uh-oh. What's with the disdain? Was that a bad idea?"

"Honestly? What happened tonight is dredging up memories of what I went through in Chicago. And it's making me sick to my stomach. Maxwell PD has a description of the car and they're looking for the guy. So can we just chill? Over, what, a cup of coffee?"

"You know what would be even better?"

"What's that?"

"Chilling over a bottle of wine."

"Mmm, I've actually got a pinot noir I've been wanting to try. Be right back."

Troy followed her into the kitchen, still unwilling to let her out of his sight. "You grab the wine while I get the glasses."

It wasn't a suggestion. It was a statement. A tilt of Chloe's head confirmed she understood that he didn't want her to be alone.

As she headed toward the refrigerator, Troy noticed her shoulders slump. Her fists were clenched, like two balls of tightly coiled yarn. While she spoke with an air of calm, she walked with an aura of defeat.

There's no way I'm leaving you tonight, he almost blurted. But if he said it out loud, Chloe would refuse his offer to stay. Tell him she'd be fine. And that she didn't want to inconvenience him.

Her Chicago PD swagger was still there—the big-city toughness that she couldn't seem to shake. But Troy knew how to play it. He'd stick around in a more subtle way. Maybe fall asleep on the couch, knowing she wouldn't have the heart to wake him. It was calculated but necessary in his effort to keep her safe.

The pair was silent as she pulled the wine from the refrigerator and a bottle of Tylenol from a drawer. He slid two glasses off the chrome rack and followed her back into the living room. A string of subjects tumbled through his head while he scrambled for a safe topic.

As soon as they settled onto the couch, Chloe swallowed down a couple of pills. Her gaze shifted from Troy to the frameless stone fireplace. His remained fixed on her. After everything she'd been through that night, she still managed to look beautiful. Her loose curls were just slightly tousled and her beige cable-knit sweater hung from her left shoulder. Traces of pink gloss still stained her lips, somehow making them even more inviting.

Cool out, Troy told himself as the rattling guilt came rushing back. Only this time it was due to his lustful thoughts.

Chloe slid in closer, as if needing the comfort of his body

next to hers. When she murmured, "I'm really glad you're here," a stir roused below his belt.

Her palm glided across the cushion and slid up his arm. The sensation of her touch brought the stir in his pants to full attention. He took a gulp of wine, hoping she hadn't noticed, despite her eyes drifting down his body.

Another long pause lingered between them. Too embarrassed to make eye contact, he stared into his glass, getting lost in the swirling burgundy liquid.

"Hey," Chloe whispered, "now it's my turn to ask. Are *you* okay?"

"I'm good," Troy lied. "Just, uh…just doing what you asked me not to do. Thinking about the case."

"I've got an idea. Why don't we do this mental exercise that I learned back in Chicago? The officers and I would practice it whenever we felt overwhelmed or needed to mentally recover from a traumatic experience."

"Okay, I'm down. Tell me about it."

Chloe set their glasses on the coffee table, then took both of his hands in hers. "All right. Turn toward me, then take a deep breath."

Troy did as he was told, watching as she closed her eyes and pulled in a deep stream of air. The sight of her breasts pushing against her sweater sent a streak of heat straight to his core.

This isn't gonna work…

"I want you to inhale slowly," Chloe continued, "using four counts in through your nose. Hold it for a few seconds, then let it out through your mouth. As you breathe, think of the most glorious place on earth that you could be right now. And imagine that you're there."

The moment his eyelids fell, visions of Chloe's bedroom sprang to mind. An image of her strolling toward the sil-

ver sleigh bed and peeling back the embroidered satin com-
forter. Pulling off her sweater and jeans. He'd bury his face in
her neck. Their lips would meet. Slowly parting before their
tongues intertwined.

"Troy?"

His eyes shot open. Chloe was leaning into him, her hand
clutching his shoulder.

"Are you okay?"

"Um…yeah—*yes*," he stammered. "I don't know what
just happened. But I…"

"I think I may have hypnotized you. I called your name
at least three times!"

"I guess that exercise of yours worked a little better than
we'd expected."

"It must have. And I didn't even get a chance to get all the
way into it. There are some grounding techniques that we
could explore, meditation practices we can try."

"Mmm-hmm," Troy uttered before emptying his glass.
"Well, your mission was accomplished during step one. Any
remnants of anxiety I'd been feeling are completely gone. So
thank you." Before she could reply, he jumped to his feet. "I
need to hit the restroom. Be right back."

Troy didn't really need to go. He just had to excuse himself from Chloe's presence before he made a move that he'd
regret.

CHLOE RAN HER hand over her legs, the roughness of her jeans
rasping against her damp palms. Troy being there, especially
after what she'd just been through, had her feeling a deep
sense of affection and appreciation. Emotions that ignited
an arousal she was desperate to extinguish. Immediately.

"I'm back," he said, slowly easing into the seat next to

hers. When he'd gotten up, there were a few inches between them. Now he was so close that his thigh pressed against hers.

A burst of heat shot through her core. She crossed her legs, squeezing them together to alleviate the insatiable throbbing. It persisted.

"How are you feeling?" Troy asked, resting his arm along the back of the couch.

Chloe squirmed against the cushion. Attempting to slip away from him, she shifted toward the side of the couch. Her shoulder blades skimmed his hardened bicep along the way. "Better."

"Are you sure? Because tonight was a lot. I was so worried about you."

She replied with a nod. He emitted an unconvinced grunt. She looked up, their eyes connecting.

"I promise you, Troy, I'm fine."

"Okay. Just making sure."

His fingertips slid across her hand and up her arm. Traveled along the back of her neck, sending a stream of tingles rippling through her center.

There was no holding back. No thoughts of Dani, or their connection being taboo. Something about the danger she'd faced left her feeling bold. Open to taking a risk for what she wanted. And in that moment, all she wanted was Troy.

He drew her in, gently pressing his mouth to hers. Chloe's breathing ceased. But as he massaged her lips, she slowly exhaled. The kiss deepened as her palm glided across Troy's abs up to his chest. Her fingers relished each indentation and every hardened muscle, the feel of his body dissolving the night's trauma.

A low moan crept up Chloe's throat as their tongues danced. Thoughts of them slipping between her sheets soothed her, stoking her desire to take his hand and lead him to the bedroom.

The titillating urge ceased when Troy suddenly pulled away. "I—I am so sorry."

"You're sorry? For what?"

"For kissing you. I shouldn't have done that. I didn't even ask first. I just…I just went in and… You've had such a rough night. You're probably feeling vulnerable. And I don't want you thinking I'm trying to take advantage of—"

"Troy," Chloe whispered, gently caressing his face. "Please. You do not have to apologize. Trust me. You're not taking advantage of me. Isn't it obvious that I want this, too?"

"It is. But still…"

Something hard vibrated against her leg.

"Ugh," he grunted, pulling his cell from his pocket.

The sensual spark buzzing within Chloe fizzled as he stared at the screen.

"That's a text from Dani. The squad hasn't had any luck tracking down the driver. But they're still searching."

"My God," Chloe moaned, her head falling into her hands. "I bet Dani regrets the day I moved back to Maxwell. My return has brought nothing but drama."

"I highly doubt that. And I, for one, am happy you're back. You've been a much-needed breath of fresh air."

"Thank you. And so have you. More than you know."

Gratitude filled his gaze as he responded to the text. While Chloe finished off her wine, her thoughts shifted back to the wild car chase. The threatening texts she'd received and the dead flower stems delivered to Jasmine. Her murder. The decapitated mannequin. Jennifer's murder. And what the killer was planning next.

The horrifying thoughts were exhausting. To the point where Chloe stood and told Troy that she needed to get some rest. She waited for him to follow her to the door. But he remained seated.

"I know you don't think I'm leaving you here alone tonight," he said. "So you may as well grab an extra pillow and blanket so I can set up shop right here on the couch."

His insistence was sexy, as was the bravado in his deep, commanding tone. Chloe almost invited him into her bedroom. But she resisted.

"I'll go grab some linens. You know where the guest bathroom is. I'll lay out towels and a toothbrush for you."

"Thanks. Appreciate it."

"No," Chloe rebutted. "All the appreciation tonight goes to you. Thank you for being here. You have no idea how much it means to me."

"Don't speak too soon. You just might get sick of me."

"Trust me, that'll never happen."

Chapter Fourteen

"Are you *sure*?" Chloe asked Michael Collins, Chicago PD's chief of police, for the third time.

"I'm positive. Trust me, I wish I could be of more assistance. But this is all I've got."

Her jaws tightened at the news. After Maxwell PD failed to link any of the evidence they'd collected at the crime scenes to a suspect, she'd rolled the dice and contacted Chief Collins. He was one of the few members of the Chicago PD that she actually trusted. Plus, he had access to inside information that most others didn't.

Chloe had feared he would ignore her email, considering the strained circumstances surrounding her retirement. *Shock* was an understatement when he'd accepted her Zoom meeting invitation.

"So you've had eyes on Justin since I've been gone?" she asked.

"I have. And he's been working nonstop double shifts. I can guarantee you he hasn't had time to take an overnight trip to Evanston, let alone spend days away committing crimes in Arizona, then make it back to Chicago as if nothing happened."

Chloe was tempted to keep pressing the chief. But judging by the taut expression on his long, slender face, he was resolute in his response.

Disappointment raged through her body like a wildfire, burning the hope that had been keeping her going. It didn't help matters that right before the Zoom meeting began, Dani had called. The threatening text messages Chloe had been receiving had been sent from a burner phone number that couldn't be traced.

"Listen," Chief Collins said, "I'll continue to keep my eyes and ears open. If anything suspicious comes up, I'll let you know. I'm sorry I couldn't be more helpful."

"No worries. Thank you for speaking with me. I really appreciate it. Hey, before you go, can I ask a quick question?"

"Of course."

"I know this isn't any of my business, but whatever happened with the Righteous Nation? Were the ringleaders I attempted to apprehend ever captured?"

Running his hand along his stubbled jawline, the chief muttered, "I hate to tell you this, but no. And just between us, I blame it all on that night you were attacked. You *had* those guys. But by the time the squad jumped in to help you, the Righteous Nation had us outnumbered. We were forced to take cover once they began shooting. Then they got away. The tactical gang unit has yet to put together another suitable sting operation. So those gang members are still at large."

"What about the money that went missing from the Reckless Assassins raid?"

"It never showed back up."

"So how did the department end up justifying that with Internal Affairs?"

"Well, since there was no proof that Detective Walters had stolen it, they believed his claim that it had been miscounted before hitting the evidence room."

In other words, it was my fault...

"I'm so sorry," Chief Collins continued. "You know, if I'm being honest, that unit hasn't been the same since you left. The leadership is lacking, the operations are disorganized and the critical thinking skills just aren't there. To put it bluntly, no one has been able to fill your shoes, Detective Grant. Your presence on this police force is truly missed."

Chloe's shoulders lifted, as if inflated with a fresh dose of energy. The chief's words had managed to rectify everything she'd been through before her career's demise.

"Thank you for that, Chief Collins. I appreciate your honesty. And, of course, your kind words."

"I'm just telling it like it is. Again, if anything comes up that I think you should know, I'll reach out. Take care of yourself, Detective Grant. And be careful out there."

"I will. Same to you."

Chloe closed her web browser, her lips spreading into a satisfied smile. Even though the meeting hadn't gotten her any closer to solving the case, she had gotten something out of it. Something that she'd desperately needed—confirmation that she had in fact been a good detective and she wasn't to blame for the operation's failure.

Grabbing her phone, she dialed Troy's number. The call went straight to voicemail. She hung up and composed a text. Right before she hit Send, a light knocking echoed behind her.

She swiveled on her cream velvet bar stool and scanned the kitchen. A series of flutters caught her eye.

Sliding off the seat and crouching down, Chloe crept toward the counter.

"What in the...?"

Flashes of metallic green dashed past the window.

Get your gun, she told herself.

Chloe wasn't playing games anymore. If someone wanted to show up to her house uninvited, they'd run the risk of being shot.

Just as she crept over to the island and grabbed her gun, a soft thud hit the windowsill. She leaped to her feet and aimed to fire.

"Ugh," Chloe groaned at the sight of a black-chinned hummingbird.

Boom boom boom!

She jolted against the granite countertop. That wasn't the sound of a pecking bird. It was a bang against the front door.

A glance at her cell showed no missed calls or texts from Troy. He was the only person who would come by her house. But never unannounced.

Gripping the gun tighter, she hugged the wall from the kitchen to the living room. Wrapped her finger around the trigger and peeked through the peephole. No one was there. Neither was the Maxwell PD surveillance vehicle that was usually parked across the street. He must've gone to lunch.

"Now I know I'm not just hearing things."

Her Glock gave her confidence. Enough to swing open the door and step onto the porch. Pivot to the right and left. No one was there.

Maybe I am *hearing things.*

Chloe stepped back into the house. Just as she grabbed the door handle, she noticed a white box propped inside her mosaic plant pot. Her stomach dropped as she searched the block again. Whoever had left the box was nowhere in sight.

Chloe's first instinct was to call Troy again. As curious as she was, the safest thing would be to have him open it.

Slamming the door shut, she rushed to the kitchen and grabbed her phone. Tried him again. The call went straight to voicemail once more.

She hung up and sent him a text.

Please call me ASAP!

After sending the message, Chloe tried Dani's office. Voicemail.

Chloe hung up, shouting, "Where in the hell is every-body!" Panic grabbed hold of her throat. She tried to inhale but choked on the fear smothering her chest.

Calm down. Take a deep breath. Maybe it's nothing. It could be something that was delivered to the wrong house. Or maybe it's a gift from the homeowners' association...

But Chloe knew better. Neither a neighbors' package nor an HOA gift would come in an unmarked box left inside her cactus planter by some weird phantom.

She checked the phone again. No calls, no texts.

Curiosity sent her feet shuffling back down the hallway and through the living room. Parting the beige wooden blinds, Chloe stared around the porch. Along the driveway. Up and down the block. Not a soul was in sight.

Her patience had run out. With her gun in hand, she slipped back out onto the landing and peered at the box. It appeared clean and intact. A shiny gold circular label sealed it shut. The package didn't look like something a deranged killer would leave.

Stop being so dramatic and just take it inside.

She grabbed the box and carried it into the kitchen. The contents were so lightweight that it practically felt empty. But when Chloe shook it, something shifted inside. Just to be safe, she slipped on a pair of protective glasses and latex gloves before peeling off the seal. The lid popped right up, revealing a wad of white tissue paper.

Chloe pulled it out and carefully unwrapped the layers.

Something slipped between the sheets and crashed against the countertop. Sliding the box to the side, she peered down at a silver dog tag. The phrase *We Serve and Protect* was engraved on one side. It was the motto of the Chicago Police Department.

Confusion hit as Chloe wondered whether the necklace was some sort of gift from an ex-coworker. She flipped the tag over and checked the other side.

Sergeant Donald Eubanks
Chicago Police Department
Badge #37112
Special Investigations Unit

Chloe had no idea who Sergeant Donald Eubanks was. She opened her laptop and searched his name. An article written in the *Chicago Sun-Times* popped up. It had been published fifteen years ago, after the sergeant died in the line of duty.

She studied his photo. Chloe was almost positive she'd never seen him before. Scanning each paragraph, she looked for some sort of connection—a reason why someone would send her his dog tag.

"There's nothing here," she murmured before reading the last paragraph.

"This is such a huge loss for our entire family," said Evelyn Eubanks, who was married to Sergeant Eubanks for almost forty years. "Donald was a hero to our son, Francis, and his wife, Carla. Whenever those two were in town, they'd stay with us for weeks on end. I don't know how we're going to get through this."

Chloe flipped the tag over again, reading each side. Obviously there was something to the delivery. She just had to figure out what.

When she reached for her phone, the tag's box fell to the floor. A balled-up index card tumbled out. She was slow to bend down and retrieve it. Her hand stiffened as she peeled back the corners. Bold capital letters scrawled in red ink distorted her vision. Squeezing her eyes shut, she counted to ten, then regained her focus.

YOU CAN RUN FROM YOUR PAST BUT YOU CAN'T HIDE FROM THE PRESENT. I'M GETTING CLOSERRR...

Chapter Fifteen

"I am at a total loss here," Chloe told Troy. "It seems like everywhere I turn, I get shut down."

He hit the accelerator, his unmarked police vehicle speeding through a yellow light while heading down Rock Canyon Road. "Don't lose hope. The answer is out there. We just have to keep putting the puzzle pieces together."

"How are we supposed to do that when none of them fit?"

It was a good question. One that Troy didn't have the answer to. Not that he'd ever tell Chloe that. With her, he always erred on the side of hope.

But he, too, was growing weary. The pair had just left the Kroger parking lot in search of evidence the team might have missed. They'd come up empty. Neither of them understood the meaning of the dog tag that had been delivered to her house. They had sent it to the crime lab and were awaiting the results. With three of their suspects having solid alibis, the list was quickly dwindling.

News of the murders had moved beyond Arizona. The case was being reported on nationally, bringing the pressure to solve it to an all-time high. Maxwell PD was exhausted, working long hours day after day in search of the suspect. The entire town was living in fear.

Chloe divulged that she was experiencing a different

level of terror considering she'd become a target. The killer's taunts were breaking her down—to the point where she had briefly considered moving away. But Troy reminded her that she was a fighter. It was time to squash her guilt for luring the killer to Maxwell and focus on getting him off the streets.

Reaching over and covering her hand with his, Troy asked, "What about Simon Grazer? Did you reach out to the executives on *The Chicago Force* and find out whether or not he's been away from the set?"

"I did. But no one's responded yet. Which is also very frustrating. I'll contact them again this afternoon."

"Good. And I know you've been down, but don't lose that determined edge of yours. The killer is bound to slip up at some point."

"I hope so…"

"I'll tell you what. Why don't we give all talk of the investigation a rest? We've done enough for today. Let's grab something to eat, go back to my place and watch a movie or something. How does that sound?"

"That sounds perfect," Chloe breathed. "My brain does need a break. Plus, I haven't eaten all day, and the last place I wanna be is my house."

Troy let up on the accelerator and pulled into the gas station. "Which is totally understandable. I just need to fill up real quick and we'll be on our way."

"While you do that, I'll scroll through some restaurants and see what looks appetizing."

"Thank you. Because waiting on you to figure out what you want to eat could take all night. So yeah. Please do get a head start."

"*Stop* it," Chloe spouted, giving his arm a playful nudge.

Surprised by her spirited reaction, Troy leaned over and

gently kissed her cheek. "I'm just glad that I was able to put a smile on your face. It's the first one I've seen today."

"Yeah, well, considering what we're dealing with, moments of joy are few and far between. But no talk of the case, remember?"

"You're right. I'll shut up. Be right back."

Troy stepped out of the car feeling lighter than he had all day. Both he and Chloe needed this night. Time to relax. Decompress. And reconnect without the weight of the case hanging over them.

A shiny black Mercedes-Benz S 63 E pulled up to the pump across from Troy's vehicle.

"Whoo," he whistled, admiring its sleek body and twenty-inch rims.

A man dressed in a custom navy suit climbed out. The setting sun's rays bounced off his Rolex's diamond bezel. His Italian leather oxfords appeared freshly polished. Compared to the casual, laid-back style of the locals, it was clear that he was an out-of-towner.

Troy watched while he strolled confidently to the other side of the car and opened the door to his tank. Just as he turned toward the pump, Chloe jumped out of the car.

"Alex?" she shrieked. "What in the hell are you doing in Maxwell?"

Troy's hand fell from the nozzle. He had to have been hearing things. Because he was certain that Chloe hadn't just called the man Alex, as in her ex from Chicago.

A woman hopped out the passenger side of his car, glaring at Chloe while wrapping an arm securely around Alex.

"Melissa, please," he said. "Don't say a word. Just get back inside the car."

"Melissa?" Chloe said, slowly approaching the couple. *"Wooow.* You know, your audacity has never ceased to amaze

me." Tossing her arms out at her sides, she turned to Troy. "Do you see who's here? All the way from Chicago, Illinois? It's my ex-boyfriend Alex and his girlfriend! You know what, Officer Miller? Suddenly, those puzzle pieces I just mentioned are starting to fall into place."

"Chloe, could you please stop making a scene?" Alex asked. "Melissa and I are just passing through town before we head back home."

"Passing through town?" Chloe mimicked, her drawl filled with sarcasm. "Why in the world would you two be passing through Maxwell, Arizona? The only tie you have to this place is me!"

"See, that's where you're wrong," Melissa shot back. "Alex and I were here in Scottsdale visiting my family."

"Oh, really? Since when do you have family in Scottsdale?"

"Um, since my parents moved here back in the late '80s."

"Yeah, right." Storming over to Troy, Chloe hissed, "How soon do you think Maxwell PD can get here to take these two in for questioning?"

"What do you mean?"

"Alex and Melissa just became our number one suspects!"

"Hold on, Chloe," Troy whispered. "We have no proof of that. We can't just take them in based on the fact that they're in town."

"Are you being serious right now? Isn't it obvious they're here to stalk and harass me, not to mention commit murder?"

"Again, we have no evidence of that. Plus, Melissa just said they'd been here visiting her family."

"And you actually believe that?"

"Listen, Chloe. I agree with you. Their presence is extremely suspicious. But right now we have nothing to go on. So let's do this the right way. Launch an investigation into their alibi. Request subpoenas on their phones to check the cell tower data. Obtain a search warrant for Alex's car's black box and Wi-Fi."

"You're right. I'm getting ahead of myself. Alex never would've agreed to come to the station anyway. He knows his rights inside and out."

"Great seeing you, Chloe!" Alex called out, flashing his neon-white veneers. "Take care of yourself."

"Go to hell, Alex!" Chloe shot back before leaning into Troy. "Those two are our prime suspects. Trust me on that."

"I do. Now we just have to prove it."

Chapter Sixteen

Maxwell PD's conference room looked like a war room, with crime scene photos, police reports, autopsy results and cell phone records scattered everywhere. Half-empty pizza boxes, drained water bottles and mugs of lukewarm coffee were strewn across the table. Laptop keyboards were clicking. Emails and texts were pinging. And Chloe, Troy and Dani were on the edge of their seats, waiting for the digital forensic investigator to join them.

Troy picked up a stack of photos and shuffled through them, each image more gruesome than the last. It wasn't that he hadn't gotten used to seeing trauma victims. He'd seen plenty while working as a paramedic in LA. But as an officer, he'd never thought he'd see such violence in his hometown.

His eyes stung at the sight of Jasmine Bailey sprawled across her front porch, blood pouring from the gruesome wounds in her chest. And Jennifer Goins, whose neck was covered in deep red bruises as her lifeless body lay twisted against the steering wheel of her car.

"Savage," Troy muttered under his breath.

"What was that?" Chloe asked.

"I said, *savage*," he repeated, sliding the pictures toward her. "The way these victims were murdered. It's diabolical."

"To put it lightly." She pushed a photo in front of him. "And let's not forget this nasty move."

Staring down at the image, Troy replied, "Oh, yeah. The decapitated mannequin doused with fake blood the killer left in your backyard."

"He definitely sent a strong message with that one..." Dani chimed in from the other end of the table.

Her voice trailed off. Troy knew where she was going with the statement. But he was glad she hadn't mentioned the *you're on my list bitch* message scrawled across the abdomen.

"Where is Chuck?" Troy asked in a bid to change the subject. "I thought he was supposed to be here by now with an update on Alex and Melissa."

"Yeah," Dani said, "me too. I'll shoot him a text now. See what's taking so long."

The moment she set the phone on the table, a ping went off near the doorway.

"I'm here!" Chuck announced from the front of the room.

The rail-thin redhead stumbled into a chair, balancing his phone and iced latte in one hand and a stack of files in the other. "Sorry I'm late. I was on a call with Chicago's Chief Collins. Chloe, he told me to tell you hello. Thanks again for putting me in touch with him. He's really cool and was a huge help. I don't know if we would've gotten ahold of Alex's car's GPS data without him."

"Trust me, I know," Chloe replied, rolling her eyes toward the ceiling. "I'm sure Alex tossed out every bit of legal jargon he could think of to try and weasel his way out of it."

"He did," Chuck confirmed. "But thanks to the gaps in federal law, it didn't work."

"Good," Dani said. "What have you got for us? Please tell me it's something relevant to this case."

He pulled reports from the files and passed them around. "I'll put it to you this way. We've definitely got some clarity on Alex and Melissa's involvement."

"So what are you saying?" Chloe asked, tearing through the pages so furiously that the paper clip flew off. "That there's proof those two are connected to the murders?"

"Not exactly. According to the GPS tracking data, they arrived in Scottsdale four days before Jennifer Goins's murder. But there's no trace of them being anywhere near the Kroger parking lot. As for Jasmine Bailey, according to their digital footprints, neither Alex nor Melissa were in the vicinity of Maxwell at the time of her murder."

"Interesting. Because, of all the places in the world they could be, we run into them in *my* hometown. The very place where I'm being stalked and harassed. Where murders are taking place that mimic my podcast..."

Tossing his hands in the air, Chuck replied, "I understand all that. But the evidence doesn't lie. And according to the records, reports and their alibis, everything checks out."

"Yeah, okay," Chloe muttered under her breath. "I'm still questioning how accurate that data is..."

Troy picked up on the shrill irritation in her tone. She didn't sound convinced of her own statement.

"So the cell phone records match up with the GPS data?" he probed.

"Yes. All the reports pretty much align perfectly with one another."

Waving her pen in the air, Dani added, "And Melissa's family? Did you find proof that she does in fact have relatives residing in Scottsdale?"

"I did. Her parents have lived there for more than thirty-five years. Surveillance footage showed Alex and Melissa visited her parents' house during the times they'd claimed to be there."

"So basically what you're saying is this was all a bust?" Chloe blurted.

"Well, I wouldn't say that. What I *would* say is we've more than likely crossed two more names off your list of suspects—"

Before he could finish, she snatched her cell off the table and stormed out of the room.

"Chloe?" Troy called out. "Chloe!"

The only response he got was the sound of her footsteps pounding the hallway.

"Please go after her," Dani told him, "and make sure she's okay."

CHLOE RUSHED THROUGH the police station's revolving doors and charged through the parking lot. Stopping at a random squad car, she unlocked her phone and barked, "Call Reva Mendell." It went straight to voicemail.

"Reva, hey. This is Chloe Grant. I know we haven't spoken in a while, but…I really need to talk to you. Can you please give me a call as soon as you get this? I need your help. Thanks. Hope to hear from you soon."

She disconnected the call, then continued scrolling through her contacts.

"Who is Reva Mendell?"

The sound of Troy's voice sent her jolting against the trunk of the car.

"Troy! You scared me. I didn't even hear you walk up."

"Yeah, well, you shook us up, too, after you ran out of the conference room. What's going on?"

"I'm tired. And frustrated. After seeing Alex and Melissa at the gas station, I was convinced we'd identified our killers. But Chuck just blew that theory right out of the water. Which means we're back at square one."

"Come here," Troy said, wrapping his arms around her as she fell against him. "Let's keep our cool. I know this isn't easy. But we're playing the long game. The case hasn't gotten solved as quickly as we'd hoped, but we'll get there."

Chloe shook her head fervently while pulling away. "Will we really? When, Troy? And how? This killer has been eluding us since day one. And he's made it no secret that I'm his main target. This may be a long game, but we're running out of time. At the rate we're going, he'll take me down before we ever get him into custody."

"I will *not* let that happen—"

"Really? And how are you gonna stop it? Because nothing you've done so far has worked."

Troy's expression fell, a mix of shock and hurt lining his gaping mouth. Before he could respond, Chloe's phone buzzed.

"Hold on," she said. "This is Reva calling me back. She's an executive producer on *The Chicago Force*."

Troy nodded, taking a few steps back.

The second her eyes met the back of his head, Chloe knew she had messed up. Gone too far. Let her emotions get the best of her. Running her words back through her mind, she cringed. She'd practically called Troy inadequate. Made it sound as if he was failing her, which meant he was failing all of Maxwell, too.

"Hello, Chloe?" someone said on the other end of the phone. "Are you there?"

"Yes! I'm here. Sorry about that."

"No worries. It's Avril, Reva's assistant."

"Oh, hey, Avril. How've you been?"

"Super busy. Things have been wild around here. Reva's on set but asked that I return your call since it sounded urgent. Is everything okay?"

"Oh, yeah. Well, no, actually. It isn't. I, um…I've actually got a private matter that I need to discuss with her. Do you know what time she'll be done shooting?"

"I don't. But I'm thinking it's gonna be a late night. Things got pretty rough earlier today during the table read, and the actors demanded that a ton of changes be made to the script. So, needless to say, there have been several major blowups and meltdowns among the writers. I mean, it's been a circus. And you can probably guess who the ringleader is…"

"Simon?"

"Of course. Honestly, things have gotten worse since you've been gone. And not to be messy, but rumor has it he's been carrying a gun to work."

"Wait—he's been *what*?" Chloe shrieked so loudly that Troy came running back over.

"I'm okay," she whispered to him. He acknowledged her with a stiff nod before walking off again.

"Yes," Avril continued. "Word is Simon's been armed on set. But you didn't hear that from me. Lucky for you, these aren't your problems anymore. Anyway, listen, why don't you send Reva an email letting her know what's going on? It'll be easier for her to check that and respond while she's working."

"Thanks, Avril. I'll do that. And hey, hang in there. I know how tough things can get."

"I know you do. We still talk about those epic battles you and Simon used to have and how you'd always win. I consider you my hero for standing up to him the way you did."

"Wow, thank you. Hearing that means a lot."

The second Chloe said her goodbyes, she ran over to Troy. "Simon's got a gun! And he's carrying it to work. That man is losing it. And his violence is escalating. I think we need to—"

"Hey!" Dani called out from the front of the station. "You two okay?"

Troy tossed her a thumbs-up.

"Can we get this meeting wrapped up?" she asked. "Chuck and I need to get back to work."

Turning to Chloe, Troy muttered, "We'd better head back inside. Let's finish this conversation later."

He set off toward the station without waiting for a response. He was noticeably slumped, as if he was carrying the weight of the world on his shoulders.

Chloe followed him in silence while replaying the conversation they'd had before her call. She wished she could take it back. He didn't deserve the harsh response after simply trying to console her.

She contemplated stopping him to apologize. But his rigid demeanor screamed that he wasn't in the mood.

Just wait, she told herself before composing the email to Reva.

Chapter Seventeen

Troy rested against the back of Chloe's couch and turned on ESPN. He was spent. Overwhelmed. And, for the second time since returning to Maxwell, questioning whether or not he should've moved back.

It pained him to admit he was failing Chloe. Failing their community. Life in LA had been so much simpler. Living in a big city meant no personal ties. No responsibility to serve those he knew thanks to his anonymity. No pressure to protect the woman he'd fallen for from some deranged killer.

Troy was still stunned after their confrontation in the parking lot. Chloe's sentiments echoed through his mind like a reel on repeat, her acerbic words stinging like a venomous bite.

The apology he'd expected never came. She had gotten lost in a frantic email exchange with Reva. While he, Dani and Chuck wrapped up the investigation into Alex and Melissa's involvement, Chloe had dived headfirst into proving that Simon was now their primary suspect.

The moment they'd arrived back at her house, she rushed into the kitchen. Chaos erupted as pots rattled, stove burners clicked and the refrigerator door slammed more times than Troy could count. He stayed put in the living room, wanting nothing more than to decompress in silence. He'd been tempted to call another officer and have him keep watch on Chloe's house so he could spend the night at his. But he didn't want to raise the tension between them any more. So he stayed, just to keep the peace.

The scent of spicy chicken wafted through the living room. Troy could recognize that aroma from a mile away. It was his favorite dish—smoky chipotle chicken chili.

He pulled a deep inhalation, the tangy blend of bell pepper and garlic inciting a rumble in his stomach. Things had been so hectic at the station that he hadn't eaten since breakfast. Neither exhaustion nor frustration could mask the fact that he was starving.

Troy muted the television at the sound of Chloe calling his name over the faint flow of running water.

"Troy!"

"Yeah?"

"Can you hear me?"

"I can. What's up?"

"Could you please come upstairs for a minute?"

"On my way…"

It took him a minute to stand, the stress of the day weighing on his stiff calf muscles. He made his way to the top of the stairs, then looked around. Chloe was nowhere in sight.

"Where are you?" he asked, sauntering toward her cracked bedroom door.

She didn't respond.

He knocked, then opened it slowly. All the lights were out. "Chloe?"

"I'm in the bathroom."

Confusion kept Troy planted in the doorway. "*Okay…* Did you need something?"

"Yes. I need for you to join me."

His confusion transformed into all-out perplexity as he

inched farther into the room. The bathroom door was almost closed. A faint beam of light shone through the crack. "Is everything all right?"

"Everything's fine. I just need to talk to you."

There was no rationalizing why Chloe would want to talk to him in the bathroom. But considering she'd been acting strangely all day, at this point, it wasn't much of a stretch.

He approached the door and stuck his head inside. The lights were turned down low, and the flicker of lavender-scented candles danced along the vanity.

"Over here," Chloe murmured.

Stepping all the way in, Troy caught sight of her and fell against the sink. She was sitting on the edge of her copper soaking tub with her legs crossed, wearing pink silk pajamas and a pink silk robe. It was partially open, revealing just enough cleavage to rouse a stir in his pants.

"What—what's going on?" he stammered, watching as she ran her fingers through the water.

"Well, after the day we had, I figured it would be nice for you to unwind in a nice warm bath before dinner. I've got a lot to catch you up on. And a few things I'd like to apologize for that I shouldn't have said. Would you mind if I gave you a nice massage?"

"No...not at all."

The minute Troy reached for his belt buckle, Chloe stood and sauntered toward him.

"No," she whispered, gently pushing his hands away. "Please, let me."

She was slow to undress him. Taking her time while unzipping his jeans and unbuttoning his shirt. It took everything in Troy not to pull her onto the floor and have his way with her. To accept the apology she had yet to officially give. Chloe had unearthed a desire deep within him that he didn't know existed. One he'd never experienced with another woman. But rather than rush to indulge, he chose to relish in it. To feed the flame until it fully ignited rather than extinguish their burgeoning fire.

When she reached for his hand, Troy followed her to the tub. The steamy water soothed his skin the moment he stepped inside. Chloe sat on the edge and poured sweet almond oil into her palm. As she ran her delicate fingers across his tight shoulders, he closed his eyes. Envisioned Chloe slipping out of her robe, the beauty of her curvaceous figure on full display. He'd grip her hips and pull her in.

"Hey," Chloe murmured, disrupting the alluring daydream.

Troy opened his eyes and smiled at Chloe. His excitement grew when she stood up. But instead of removing her robe and joining him, she leaned forward and whispered "I'm sorry for what I said earlier" in his ear before kissing him softly on the lips. "Enjoy your bath, and we'll talk later."

Chapter Eighteen

Troy turned off the car engine and rocked his head against the headrest. He stared straight ahead, overwhelmed by the haunting canopy of blue spruce firs and bristlecone pine trees nestled within the Great Blue Heron Nature Preserve.

Despite being located an hour outside of Maxwell, the preserve was still under the town's jurisdiction. Troy had gotten them there as fast as he could. Judging by the number of cop cars surrounding him and Chloe, the rest of the squad had already arrived.

A low moan prompted him to turn to her. She was slumped down in the passenger seat, visibly shaken while scanning the area.

"Here we go again," she muttered. "This is unreal…"

The sight of her quivering chin was unnerving. But her behavior wasn't surprising considering the reason for their visit.

The pair had just sat down for lunch at Sweet Maple Café when Troy's phone rang. It was the call they'd both been dreading. There had been another murder.

Hikers who'd been exploring Great Blue Heron's lush, scenic trails stumbled upon a dusty navy blue suitcase, half buried near a fallen tree. Curiosity lured them to it. The group debated whether to check it out or call the police. One overzealous trekker dropped to his knees and tore it open, convinced they'd discovered a bundle of hidden money.

According to Dani, the moment that zipper was released, a pungent odor seeped through the lid. Most of the hikers backed away in disgust. But the man who'd opened the bag kept going. Peeled off the duct tape wrapped securely around black garbage bags. Ripped open the plastic and peered at the contents. Then fell onto his back when he realized they were human body parts.

A pair of bloody calves were piled on top of a torso. The feet were shoved into one corner of the suitcase while the head was in another. The arms had been broken and shoved into crevices between each thigh.

The victim was female, extremely petite and, from what law enforcement could tell, somewhere between her late twenties and early thirties.

Bzzz...

Troy grabbed his cell and checked the notification. "That's Dani, wondering where we are. I'll let her know we're heading up to the trail."

"All right," Chloe rasped, her flat tone almost robotic.

"Are you sure you're up for this? Because if you aren't, I can go up alone while you wait here in the—"

"Of course I'm up for it. Why wouldn't I be?"

Troy didn't answer the question for fear of upsetting her further. "Okay, then. Let's go find out what we're dealing with here."

They covered themselves with protective gear before entering the preserve. Rolling slopes and marshy depressions covered the forest's floor, making the climb more challenging than they'd expected. The pair struggled to maintain their balance while forging through the dense sagebrush shrubs and bigtooth maples' low-hanging branches. Luckily, both Troy and Chloe had dressed casually for their lunch outing.

His sturdy sneakers and her combat boots helped them up the steepening incline.

As he held on to Chloe's arm to help steady her, Troy noticed his limbs growing heavy. Each step became more labored than the last, as if he was rooted to the ground. The tough trek wasn't the only cause of his burden. It was the stress of knowing they'd failed to solve the case before yet another murder had occurred.

Despite being surrounded by a team of great officers, Troy continued to carry the responsibility of capturing the killer alone. The thought of Chloe being attacked, his inherent need to protect his hometown... Those emotions were more prevalent than ever. And one thing was for certain. Time was running out and Maxwell PD was on the losing end of the investigation.

"Watch out for the rodents and frogs," Chloe warned. "And, of course, the rattlesnakes."

"Oh, trust me. My eyes are wide-open."

Yellow caution tape had been wrapped around the tree trunks looming ahead. The blur of white hazmat suits was jarring, disrupting the preserve's natural beauty. Fellow officers walked the perimeter, taking photos and scouring the ground for evidence.

As they approached the scene, Chloe held on to Troy tighter. Terror widened her eyes. He covered her hand with his, mad at himself for not insisting she wait in the car. But she never would've gone for that. Fearful or not, she was determined to help apprehend the killer.

"Hey, guys!" Dani called out. "Over here!" She was standing underneath a massive white pine tree next to the suitcase. "Can you believe this? Another one."

"No, I cannot," Troy said. "*We* cannot. Sorry it took us so long to get here. We were in the middle of lunch, and the restaurant was packed, there was a long wait and…"

Realizing he was rambling, Troy stopped himself and stared down at the body. The sight was gruesome—so surreal that it appeared more like a Halloween prop than an actual human being.

Bloodstained limbs were piled haphazardly on top of one another. They appeared fresh, as if the murder had occurred recently. The victim's intestines spilled from her torso. The head was tilted slightly to the side, with curly black hair matted against her scalp. A large wound surrounded by gray-and-white matter was splayed near her right temporal region.

"I need a minute," Chloe choked out, closing her eyes and pulling away.

Before Dani could say a word, Troy shot her a discreet head nod. She got the message and let Chloe be.

"How soon do you think we can get an ID on the victim?" he asked his sister.

"Soon, I hope. We're calling around to see if we can use a nearby police department's Rapid DNA machine since ours is on back order. If not, it might take a while. In the meantime, we're checking the database for missing-persons reports."

Troy took another glance at the mutilated body. "I wonder if the crime occurred out here. And if the medical examiner was able to tell from the marks on the severed limbs what type of tool may have been used. Was it a saw, or a machete, or maybe a chain saw?"

"Judging by the pool of blood gathered near that ponderosa pine to the left of us," Dani said, "I'm thinking the crime did occur out here. But the medical examiner is going to perform a tool-mark analysis once the body is transferred to the morgue. He'll look for any striations in the bones, and that'll help determine what type of instrument was used."

Chloe gradually pivoted on her heels, her eyes directly on Dani. "I'd suggest the medical examiner leave the victim and suitcase intact during the transfer to the morgue."

"He will. We don't want to run the risk of contaminating the evidence out here any more than the hiker already did by tearing open the suitcase and plastic bags." Dani pointed toward the collection kit in Chloe's hand. "You don't happen to have magnetic powder and casting silicone for fingerprint lifting, do you?"

"I do. Those are two of my most utilized supplies."

"Oh, good. Would you mind if I use them to try and lift some prints off the luggage? I accidentally brought the wrong color powder and clear tape instead of a rubber compound. Neither of those are gonna do the trick."

"Of course," Chloe told her before popping open the kit.

Troy tossed his sister a look. He knew Dani was lying. She carried an array of print-lifting materials on her at all times. But he didn't say a word. He knew what she was doing—attempting to shift Chloe's mood and pull her into the investigative fold.

After grabbing the items from her kit, Chloe eyed the suitcase. "Dani, I know you're busy managing the scene. I can search for prints while you do your thing. If you want…"

"Really? That would be a huge help, actually. Are you sure you don't mind?"

"Not at all."

Giving his sister a discreet wink of thanks, Troy added, "I'll stay with Chloe and help out however I can. Unless you need me elsewhere."

"No, no. You and Chloe should team up on this. I won't be too far away. Just give me a holler if you stumble on anything interesting."

"Will do."

Chloe had already begun sprinkling powder along the suitcase handle.

"You good?" Troy asked her.

"As good as I can be under the circumstances. I'm just wondering who this victim is and how she's connected to me."

"Maybe she isn't. Maybe this murder is random. Most people wouldn't know that this nature preserve is part of Maxwell PD's jurisdiction, including some of our own townspeople. Plus, you haven't released a new podcast episode in weeks. So this killing just might be unrelated."

"I wish that were true, Troy. But, unfortunately, it isn't."

"What do you mean?"

"I recorded a bonus episode early on about a woman in New York whose ex-fiancé had shot her in the head. In the right temple, no less, just like this victim appears to have been. Her body was dismembered, stuffed inside a suitcase and buried in Adirondack Park. So this is definitely connected. I'm telling you, the killer's message is getting louder. And he's getting closer."

The words imploded inside his chest. The crime itself was brutal enough. But the thought of Chloe being next crushed him.

Chapter Nineteen

Chloe leaned against the Uber's tinted window, the bright morning sun warming her face. She pulled in a long puff of Chicago's crisp, familiar air. Waited for the breath to calm the jitters buzzing through her stomach like a frenzy of bees. It didn't.

She turned to Troy and grabbed his hand. *Maybe this wasn't such a good idea*, she almost blurted.

But then Chloe noticed the awe in his gaze as he stared out at the magnificent skyline. The horizon appeared more spectacular than usual. Maybe it was the way the sun reflected off the mirrored downtown high-rises. Or the fact that she hadn't seen it in months. Either way, Chloe could barely enjoy it, as she was laser focused on the mission at hand.

After her email exchange with Reva, she'd decided that the only way they'd get some answers would be to return to Chicago. Get on the front line. See what was really going on with Simon and the gun he'd allegedly been toting—especially now that they had found a shell casing tucked between the victim's dismembered limbs.

The only person who'd actually seen his weapon on the set of *The Chicago Force* was his assistant. She was the one who'd told Avril about it. Chloe hoped that gun would be the link that chained everything together.

When she told Troy they needed to travel to Chicago and get proof that Simon was in possession of the gun, he questioned how they'd accomplish that.

"Reva sent me a schedule of all the outdoor shoots happening next week. You and I are going to sneak onto the set, remaining on the outskirts, of course, and see what we can see."

"What do you expect? For Simon to just stand out in the open waving his gun in the air?"

"Knowing him? Yes. I do."

Convincing Troy to join her in Chicago had been the easy part. It was Dani who'd required hard persuasion. She didn't want two of her best investigators away at the same time. Chloe had promised they'd only be gone a couple of days. Only then did Dani give them the green light.

The touch of Troy's hand against her thigh pulled Chloe from her thoughts.

"How much longer until we get to the set?" he asked.

"We're almost there."

"I really wish we didn't have to leave town so soon. And I hate that my first visit to this great city is wrapped up in a murder investigation."

"Yeah, me too. Once we solve this case, we'll take another trip here just for fun."

"Is that a promise?"

"Yes, that's a promise."

Troy's head jerked from right to left when the car entered an underground roadway. "Wait—where are we going? Gotham City?"

"Not quite. This is Lower Wacker Drive. It's where *The Chicago Force* is filming today."

"Humph, okay," he replied, alarm wrinkling his expression as he stared out the window.

His reaction **didn't surprise** Chloe. The multilevel under-pass was a notoriously eerie subterranean world of sorts. Its dark, winding streets were gritty and remote. Even the most well-traveled Chicagoans avoided the disarming thoroughfare. But there was no denying that it made for great television.

A fleet of trailers and steel barriers appeared in the distance. Bright LED lights hung from tripods, shining down on a flurry of activity. Crew members shuffled through high-definition cameras while the cast sat in a row of director's chairs, scripts in hand.

"Excuse me," Chloe said to the driver. "Would you mind letting us out here, please?"

"Here?" the driver asked, quickly pulling into a nearby loading dock. "Are you sure, ma'am? According to the address of your destination, you're going to Urban Kayaks. It's along the Riverwalk, which is a bit of a ways away."

Chloe was already halfway out the car before replying, "I know. I just used that as a point of reference. This is fine. Thank you!"

She led Troy toward a graffiti-infested doorway and hid inside the alcove. Covering her nose with her scarf, she ignored the stench of garbage drifting from filthy dumpsters and hot steam shooting up from manholes lining the pavement.

"It is absolutely disgusting down here," Troy mumbled from behind his hand. "This is not the part of Chicago I'm used to seeing in the movies."

"It is if you've ever watched *The Blues Brothers* or *The Dark Knight*."

He pointed toward a crowd of onlookers who had gathered along a steel barrier near a staged car wreck. "So now that we're here and you've scoped out the scene, what's the game plan?"

"Well, I was texting with Reva on the way here. She suggested we try and blend in with the bystanders and record whatever we can. Of course, I won't address her directly or make my presence known."

"Sure. But are we allowed to record while they're filming?"

"No, which means I'll have to be extremely discreet and creative. You ready to go in?"

"I am. Let's do it."

Chloe pulled a black baseball cap out of her tote and slipped it onto her head. She linked arms with Troy, and they made their way toward the set, strolling and laughing as if they were in the middle of a conversation. She adjusted the cap's brim, covering her eyes while squeezing through the spectators.

"This is a good spot," Chloe said. "I can pretty much see everything."

"Any sign of Simon?"

"Not yet. But according to Reva, he's here."

Chloe folded her arms, her muscles trembling as adrenaline shot through her body.

"Places, everyone!" the assistant director called out.

The stars of the show, Allen Wright and Emily Dunn, positioned themselves next to one of the wrecked cars.

"You got your phone ready to film?" Troy asked.

"My thumb is hovering over the record button as we speak."

"Quiet on set!" the assistant director yelled. Several moments passed while he waited for the crowd to settle down. "And—"

Before he could yell *action*, someone said, "Please read

the lines as they were written and not how you *think* they should've been written this time, Emily!"

An audible gasp swept across the set. All eyes turned toward the cluster of director's chairs. One man in particular was pointing at the lead actress. His dyed, sandy-brown comb-over was blowing in the wind. Despite the chilly temperature, he was wearing a red tank top that showcased his fleshy biceps.

Just as Chloe nudged Troy, Emily shot back, "That reminder wasn't necessary, Simon! I read it just as it was written during the last take, in case you missed it."

Several onlookers broke into applause before security shushed them.

"And we've now got eyes on public enemy number one," Troy said.

"Didn't take long for him to get started, did it?"

"Not at all."

Chloe glared across the set at Simon. She imagined charging through the barricades and slapping the smug expression off his weather-beaten face.

"Be cool," Troy whispered, wrapping an arm around her. "I can feel the anger coming off your body."

"I'll try."

Allen whispered something in Emily's ear. She nodded, rolling her sinewy neck and shoulders before lifting her frowning lips.

The sight was a stinging reminder of the drama Simon kept up back when Chloe still worked on the show. All the consoling among cast and crew members as a result of his bad behavior.

"That man is something else," Troy said. "How does he manage to keep his job?"

"Two words—Emmy nominations. *The Chicago Force*

has won several awards, and the executives believe it's all thanks to Simon's writing."

The assistant director raised a hand in the air. "Okay, people. Let's try this again. Quiet on set, please."

As a hush fell over the crowd, Chloe turned to Simon, who was shooting visual daggers in Emily's direction. But he remained silent this time.

"And...*action*!"

Allen pulled on a pair of blue latex gloves, popping them against his wrist. "I can guarantee you this crash is a result of illegal street racing."

"Either that," Emily said, peering inside a banged-up yellow Dodge Challenger, "or the driver was high on Vitamin X, or maybe both—"

"Vitamin *E*, damn it!" Simon roared before stomping toward Emily. "Vitamin E! Why the hell can't you get that through your thick head? Or are you out of your mind?"

Chloe's hand shook as she held the phone close to her chest while recording the confrontation.

"Who cares, Simon?" Emily yelled back. "They're both slang for Molly, and the term Vitamin X is more authentic than Vitamin E. Plus, that's the term used more frequently on the street!"

"Oh, so what are you, a drug dealer now?"

The exchange intensified as Simon stood inches away from Emily, waving his arms in the air as if he might hit her.

"Security!" she screamed over his shoulder. "Can someone please come and get this maniac away from me?"

Troy bent down and eyed Chloe's cell. "Please tell me you're getting all this."

"Every bit of it. I'm just waiting for that gun to make an appearance."

Two men clad in black attire and neon-orange vests rushed

onto the set. One of them stepped in between Simon and Emily while Allen pulled her away.

"Hey, everyone?" the director called out. "Let's take a break."

Emily's team swooped in and whisked her off. She was doubled over in tears, barely able to climb the stairs leading to her trailer. Simon began arguing back and forth with the director and security. One of the men took hold of his wrist, urging him to walk off the set.

"Get off of me!" Simon insisted. Spit flew from his mouth as he jerked his arm from the man's grip. He spun around and stared into the crowd, his eyes darting wildly from person to person. "What the hell are you all looking at? Hey, you! Are you *recording* me?"

Chloe had been so wrapped up in the footage that she didn't realize Simon was looking directly at her.

"Do you see this?" Simon asked the security guards. "You all are so busy harassing me that you're not even doing your jobs. Fans are not allowed to record while we're filming!"

Quickly shoving the phone in her pocket, Chloe grabbed Troy's hand. Just as she turned to leave, Simon howled, "Hey, get back here! I know you." He pushed one of the guards in her direction. "That's Chloe Grant. She should *not* be here!"

Chloe froze. Debated whether she should run off or face her arch nemesis.

It's a free country. Face him...

She held her head high, replying, "Yep, it's me, Simon. Chloe Grant. And why am I not allowed to be here?"

"Take her phone!" he snapped at the guard. "And erase that illegal footage she just recorded. Now!"

"I'm sorry, sir," the man told him. "But I can't do that."

"Well, if you won't, then I will."

Simon jumped over the steel barricade and pushed through

the crowd. The guard charged after him. But Simon was like a rabid animal, desperate to get to Chloe's phone. Right before he reached her, Troy stepped in the way.

"I'd suggest you walk away, man," Troy told him. "Trust me on that."

Simon's five-nine frame appeared minuscule next to Troy's overpowering physique. He leaned to the side, glaring past Troy and directly at Chloe. "This isn't over. I'm gonna call the police. You know, the force that chewed you up and spit you out? So don't do anything stupid with that footage. Unless you want to face felony charges for trespassing and invasion of privacy and get thrown in jail!"

"Yeah, I don't think that's how it works," Chloe shot back.

"Come on," Troy told her. "Let's just go."

"Yeah, listen to your little boyfriend and get the hell out of here!"

"Ignore him and keep walking," Troy advised.

Chloe pulled her phone back out, her fingers trembling as she ordered an Uber. "Now do you see why I think Simon's our main suspect?"

"Oh, for sure. So what now?"

"We need to show this video to Chief Collins. Let him know that Simon is possibly armed and definitely dangerous."

Chapter Twenty

"This is fine right here, thanks."

The Uber driver pulled over alongside a chain-link fence. Chloe hopped out but Troy just sat there, staring out at the dismal alleyway. Redbrick buildings cast shadows over dingy trash bins. The asphalt was riddled with weed-filled cracks. Cars were parked haphazardly next to peeling garage doors. It had to be the wrong location.

"Are you coming?" Chloe asked him.

"Yeah, I just… Are you sure this is where we're supposed to be?"

"I'm positive. This is the police precinct where I used to work."

The driver's phone dinged for a second time, alerting him that he had another pickup.

"Sorry," Troy uttered before finally climbing out of the car.

"I just texted Chief Collins," Chloe said. "Asked if he'd come around to the back and meet us."

"You don't want to meet with him inside the precinct?"

"Absolutely not. I've already gotten word that Justin is here. I do not want to see him."

"Understood." Troy hesitated, choosing his words carefully before proceeding. "So, what are your expectations of Chief Collins after you show him that video?"

"What do you mean?"

"What I mean is, how are you going to convince him that Simon's worth looking into?"

"Isn't this recording I have of him behaving like a complete maniac and threatening me enough? Not to mention he's armed—"

"Allegedly," Troy interjected.

Waving him off, Chloe huffed, "Why would his assistant lie about something like that? And you know what else? I bet he doesn't even have a concealed carry license! Not to mention employees aren't allowed to bring firearms to work. Should I go on?"

Leave it alone, Troy told himself. But Chloe pressed on, saying, "I'm listening," while folding her arms expectantly.

He didn't have the heart to tell her there might not be enough evidence against Simon to warrant a probe. But maybe he was wrong. She was a former Chicago detective who'd maintained a good rapport with the chief. That could be enough to launch an investigation.

"I just hope Chief Collins will be open to your request."

Chloe responded with a shrug. If it was her way of trying to appear unbothered, it didn't work, as her wary expression was a dead giveaway.

"Is that your phone I hear buzzing?" Troy asked.

"Yep. It's the chief. He's on his way out."

Her arms fell by her sides as she paced the ramp leading up to the precinct's back door. She leaned against the rusted green banister, wringing her hands while moving her lips as if practicing what to say.

Please let this go well, Troy thought right before the door swung open. A tall, burly man came lumbering out. He and Chloe embraced before she led him back down the ramp.

"Troy, this is Chief Collins. Chief, this is Officer Troy Miller. He and I are working together on the serial-killer case back in Maxwell."

"Nice to meet you, Officer Miller," the chief said, extending a hand.

"It's nice to meet you as well, sir. I've heard a lot of great things about you."

"Same here. I'm sorry about what you're going through back home. According to Chloe, she thinks I might be able to help out in some way." The chief peered down both ends of the alleyway. "You know, you two are more than welcome to come inside and talk in my office. There's no need for us to hide out back here. Detective Grant, I'm sure plenty of your old squad members would love to see—"

"I'd rather not," Chloe interrupted. "I'm already on edge after what just happened with Simon on the set. The last thing I need is to run into that ex-partner of mine and get into another altercation."

"I highly doubt that would happen. Detective Walters hasn't always made the best decisions, but he's dealt with the consequences of his past actions. I believe he learned his lesson. He's actually been on the straight and narrow ever since that incident at the Righteous Nation's headquarters."

"Chief, now that you're no longer my boss, I can tell you that you're too nice. *Way* too nice. You give people grace when they've done nothing to deserve it."

"Yeah, and I provide help to those I am under no obligation to assist, too."

"Touché," Chloe quipped before they broke into laughter.

Troy stepped to the side, slipping his hands in his jeans' back pockets. Seeing Chloe in her element was cool, yet bittersweet. The level of respect Chief Collins still maintained for her was evident. But it was unfortunate how corruption had forced her out of the department. Chicago PD had lost a good one.

Their loss, however, was a win for Maxwell. It was good having her back home, as Chloe's return was beginning to feel a lot like the path to Troy's future.

"Look, Detective," Chief Collins said, "I've got a ton of work to do. The department is slammed right now. So let me see this video you shot so we can talk next steps and I can get back to my desk."

Chloe launched the video and turned up the volume. As it began to play, Troy kept his eyes on the chief to see his reaction. He remained stone-faced throughout. When it ended, he stared blankly at the screen.

"Do you need to see it again?" Chloe asked.

"No, I think I've seen enough. Is that all you've got or did you record something else?"

"No, that's it. But isn't that enough?"

"Enough to do what?" Chief Collins asked.

And this is what I was afraid of... Troy thought.

"Enough to go down to the set and question Simon about his threatening behavior. Question the cast and crew members to find out who else is being subjected to his abuse. More importantly, look into whether or not he has in fact been carrying a gun. According to one of the executive producers on the show, Simon's been away off and on. That means he could in fact be traveling to Maxwell to commit these crimes, then make it back to Chicago in time for work."

"Detective Grant, listen to me. If Simon's coworkers aren't filing charges or complaints against him, then there's really nothing I can do. He didn't physically assault anyone in that video. And there's no proof that he's in possession of a gun.

Speaking of which, have any of his coworkers actually *seen* the weapon? Or is this just hearsay?"

"I was told that his assistant saw it," Chloe muttered while typing away on her phone. "I'll see if she had solid proof. But in the meantime, just know that our latest victim had been shot in the head before her body was dismembered and stuffed inside a suitcase. Luckily, a shell casing was recovered at the scene. If Simon does own a gun, I'd love for Forensics to run a ballistics test to see if the markings on that casing match up with his firearm."

"Okay, well, let's not get ahead of ourselves. And keep in mind I've got unsolved homicide investigations piled high on my desk. Armed robberies. Drug transactions. Carjackings. And the list goes on. You're not new to this, Detective. You worked here alongside me for years. I can't take time away from those cases to chase after this, this... I honestly can't even call it a lead."

As cool as it was outside, Chloe's forehead was now covered in perspiration. "I cannot believe I came all this way, got into an altercation with Simon, got proof of his foolery on video, and it's still not enough. I am convinced that man is out to get me. I'm telling you, Chief, he's our prime suspect—"

"All right, all right," Chief Collins interjected, clutching one of her hands. "Let me do some digging. Reach out to some of my contacts and see what I can find. If anything comes up, I'll let you know. And this stays between us. I'm doing it off the record, as a favor to you."

"*Thank* you," Chloe replied, giving him a big bear hug. "Mum's the word."

"You're welcome. Now, you two get out of here. Officer Miller, it was nice meeting you. Be sure to take good care of my girl and keep her safe."

"Same here, sir, and will do." Troy offered him a hand but ended up in a bear hug as well.

"Detective Grant, I'll be in touch. Stay out of trouble!"

Once Chief Collins was back inside the precinct, Troy led Chloe toward the end of the alleyway. "So what now? More investigative work? Or lunch and a quick tour of the Gold Coast?"

"After the morning we've had? Option B for sure. I'll call a car. We'll do steaks and cocktails, a walking tour to burn some calories and see some sights, then head back to the hotel to decompress and debrief."

"Sounds like a plan," Troy told her, relieved that, for the first time since they'd landed, he was finally coming down off an anxiety-ridden high.

Chapter Twenty-One

By the time Chloe and Troy arrived back at the hotel, they were both spent. The day hadn't gone as planned. Their time on the set of *The Chicago Force* had ended way sooner than she'd expected, as had her meeting with Chief Collins. It was a lot to take in. So much that Chloe had pushed it all out of her mind and allowed herself to enjoy the city.

She and Troy had gone to RPM Steak and indulged in succulent roasted diver scallops drizzled with tangy yuzu butter. Shredded kale salads adorned with smoky shiitake mushrooms and crispy bites of bacon. Tender rib-eye fillets and whipped blue cheese potatoes. Then topped it all off with a bottle of cabernet sauvignon and coffee crème brûlée.

They walked it off while window-shopping along Michigan Avenue. After an architectural boat tour along the Chicago River, they agreed to call it a day and get some rest before flying out the next morning.

When booking the trip, Chloe and Troy had thought it would be best to stay in separate hotel rooms. "For professional reasons," they'd said. To keep their focus. And put their all into the investigation. But since Chloe and Troy had booked the trip at the last minute, the hotel had limited availability. So they ended up having to settle on one room with one bed.

After their latest victim was discovered, Chloe and Troy

hadn't had an opportunity to discuss their relationship. But what was understood didn't need to be spoken. Their feelings for one another were apparent. For now, however, they needed to focus on the business at hand—capturing the killer.

Once they'd returned to the hotel, they kicked off their shoes and stretched out across the comfy king mattress.

"Hey, I've been thinking," Troy said. "Maybe it's time for us to switch gears. Try something different with this investigation, since nothing we've done so far has provided any real leads."

"I'm all for that. Got any ideas?"

"I do. The Melodic Music Festival is happening next weekend. We should go. Scope out the scene. See if anything stands out that might relate to the case."

"But that festival takes place over two hours away in the middle of Peyote Valley, doesn't it?"

"It does," Troy confirmed, pulling up the event details on his phone. "I figured since our last two victims regularly attended that music festival—according to their Instagram accounts, at least—it would be worth a shot. Plus, it's a huge event that draws crowds from Arizona, California, Nevada, Colorado…all over the West, really. The alcohol and drug use is rampant. Which means attendees are wide-open and vulnerable. Their guards are down. They're all about having a good time and not thinking of their safety. And maybe someone could share some information. What does that sound like to you?"

"A playground for a killer looking for his next victim."

"Exactly. So, what do you think? Is it worth checking out?"

"It couldn't hurt," Chloe said with a shrug. "At this point I'm open to trying anything that'll help solve this investigation."

"Cool. I'll order the tickets. In the meantime, why am I already thinking about food again?"

"Well, we did exert a lot of energy on that tour of the city."

"That's true. But one thing's for sure—I'm not leaving this room again until it's time to head to the airport in the morning. So we'll be ordering room service for dinner. If that's okay with you."

Chloe grabbed the menu off the nightstand. "That's fine with me. You know, after we left the set, then talked to Chief Collins, I started thinking this trip was a bust. But it wasn't. The video and chat with the chief prompted an investigation into Simon's behavior. So, all in all, it was worth it."

"Oh, yeah. It was definitely worth it. If for nothing else, that rib-eye fillet. *Mmm...*"

"Stop it," she said, playfully swatting his arm.

Rolling over onto his side, Troy clutched his bicep. "Ow! Come on, I'm kidding! Obviously I'm glad we got something out of this trip. But in all honesty, lying here next to you will be my biggest highlight."

His words eased the adrenaline that had been coursing through her body all day. "That is such a sweet thing for you to say, Troy. Thank you."

"Of course. I mean every word of it. Now, how are you feeling after the day we had?"

"Still a little wired. But better. Glad that the worst of this trip is behind us."

"And the best of it is still in front of us..."

Troy ran his fingertips along her arm and rested them against her palm. She quivered, his touch sending a tingling sensation straight to her center. Their eyes and fingers locked simultaneously. Sensual energy surged between them.

"What's on your mind?" he asked, tucking a lock of curls behind her ear.

"You wanna know the truth?"

"Of course."

"Kissing you."

"Hmm, interesting."

"Why is that?" Chloe asked.

"Because we're thinking the exact same thing."

Troy slid his finger underneath her chin, running it along the curve. She raised her head as his knuckle gently traced her jaw. It wandered along her earlobe, then down her slender neck, sending her body shivering beneath his touch.

For a brief moment, her mind drifted back to the investigation. What Chief Collins would uncover. And whether they'd get to the killer before he got to her.

"Hey," Troy whispered, his thumb stroking her forehead. "You're doing that thing you do."

"What thing?"

"The same thing you did that very first day we reconnected back in Maxwell. You know, getting in your head rather than being in the moment. What's on your mind?"

Chloe's gaze lifted, meeting his curious stare. "My mind did wander off for a minute. I was thinking about the case again, and…"

"Listen. When it comes to the investigation, we've done everything we can. At least for the time being. You deserve a break from it. We both do. So do me a favor, okay? Just for tonight, let's take advantage of the fact that we're here. Together. Alone and away from Maxwell. We can pick up the case tomorrow. As for tonight? It's all about you and me."

The words flowed through her ears like a sweet melody, pushing all thoughts of the investigation from her mind while curling her lips into a smile. "I like the sound of that."

Troy skimmed the small of her back and pulled her closer, slipping between her legs. She reached down, his thick arousal hardening within her grasp. Chloe's eyelids fluttered as he sprinkled her face with delicate kisses. Each one made its own statement. His attraction toward her. His appreciation of her. His fondness and concern. The words didn't need to be spoken. They could be felt in each tender touch of his lips.

When their mouths finally met, Chloe moaned, releasing the last remnants of stress that had been plaguing her. Not only did she want this, but she needed it. Needed Troy's physical touch to reinforce that she was safe. That she wasn't in this alone. And that this time, she had a true partner by her side.

The pair couldn't pull each other out of their clothes fast enough. The moment Chloe's soft breasts spilled from her bra, Troy cupped them in his hands while teasing her lips with his tongue. Her legs straddled his hips as he slithered down the bed. Running her hands along his hardened biceps, she pulled him toward her. The urgency was unbearable. Chloe couldn't wait any longer.

"Are we really doing this?" he breathed, his erection stabbing her inner thigh.

"Yes, we're really doing this."

When her back arched, Troy slid inside her. She closed her eyes, biting down on his neck while moans vibrated against his chest. For the first time in a long time, Chloe felt content. And at peace. All while being wrapped in an irresistible layer of bliss.

Giving herself to Troy hadn't been a rash decision. Every interaction between them had led up to this moment. She'd taken a huge leap of faith being intimate with him. Trusting him with her heart, believing that he was different. Chloe was convinced he was a good man with a pure soul—someone worthy of receiving the most sacred part of her.

"Please don't mess this up," she whispered, not realizing she'd spoken the words aloud.

As he slowed his stroke, Troy's lips caressed her earlobe, and he murmured, "I've been waiting on this moment for years. Trust me, the last thing I'd ever do is ruin it."

Chapter Twenty-Two

"I'm too old for this," Chloe muttered as she and Troy approached the Melodic Music Festival gates. "The heavy bass is already bursting my eardrums. It's hot. It's packed..."

"You'll be fine. And we don't have to stay out here all day. We'll just scope the scene and see what's what. If nothing stands out, we can leave."

A security guard scanned their wristbands and patted them down. After walking through a metal detector, they were finally allowed onto the festival grounds.

The spacious field was filled with hundreds of attendees dressed in skimpy boho-chic gear, from bright floral minidresses and crocheted crop tops to tiny, frayed denim skirts and fringed bikini tops. Most of the men were shirtless, with cargo shorts and distressed jeans being their gear of choice.

Chloe blended right in with the crowd in her burnt-orange maxidress, as did Troy, who'd chosen a black tank and camouflage chinos. While she'd expected a younger crowd, guests appeared to run the gamut, from teenagers to a few seniors sprinkled throughout the crowd.

"I'm surprised we had to go through a pat down *and* a metal detector just to get in here," Chloe said. "That's not a good sign."

"I've heard security has increased in recent years thanks

to all the substance abuse, which you know leads to rowdy behavior. People attempting to bring weapons onto the grounds, fights breaking out..."

"This crowd doesn't look like the type." Spinning a 360-degree turn, she took in everything around her. "Where should we even start?"

"I have no idea. There's so much going on out here."

Three large stages and two smaller ones had been set up across the field. Food vendors, merchandise tents, art installations and carnival rides were scattered in between. The performance lineup was chock-full of pop and R & B artists who'd be taking the stages throughout the day.

"Maybe we can walk around for a bit and scope out the scene," Chloe suggested. "Then head over to stage two. Victoria Monét is scheduled to perform in about forty-five minutes. There should be a good-sized crowd gathered once she goes on."

"Let's do it. And hopefully we'll stumble upon a seafood stall selling lobster rolls along the way."

As they strolled through the throngs of people, Chloe resisted the urge to grab hold of Troy's hand. It was easy to forget they were there on business. An upbeat vibe filled the air while concertgoers ate, drank, laughed and danced to harmonious blends of jazz and funk. Chloe's *I'm too old for this* energy shifted as her hips swayed to the music. When she noticed Troy's eyes on her, she couldn't resist snaking her waist a little more seductively.

"You'd better cut it out," he quipped, despite the smirk on his face saying otherwise.

The soft curve in his lips prompted Chloe to grab hold of his arm. "And if I don't?"

A throaty chuckle oozed through his sensuous grin. "Keep playing with me and you're gonna find out."

"*Tuh.* Don't threaten me with a good time."

When her hand slid down his arm, their fingers intertwined. Troy's touch, his thick, firm hands swallowing hers, sent a stream of tingles bursting through her chest.

"You smell that?" he asked, tilting his head to the sky while pulling in a long breath of air.

Chloe did the same, the aroma prompting a growl in the pit of her stomach. "I smell a lot of things. Barbecued ribs, French fries, tacos, beer... Which are you referring to?"

"The sweet, rich, buttery scent of lobster rolls."

With a squeeze of his hand, he changed directions and led her toward a row of colorful food stalls.

"See?" Troy said, pointing toward an ocean-blue stand with waves painted across the front. "I knew it. There's the Latest Catch. Have you been to their restaurant?"

"No, I haven't. But I've heard great things about it. Judging by the line, it's got to be good."

"Well, we've some time on our hands before Victoria Monét's set starts. Let's find out if all the hype is true."

As the pair took their position at the back of the line, Victoria's band hit the stage. They began adjusting the speaker volume while singing, "Check, check, one two three, check," into the mics. Guitar strings plucked while high notes flowed from the keyboard. After three hits to the rim of a snare drum, the band broke into Victoria's "We Might Even Be Falling in Love" interlude.

The crowd went wild. Arms flew into the air as everyone belted out the lyrics.

"Ooh, I love this song," Chloe gushed before singing a verse.

Chloe had been so busy bouncing to the music that she hadn't noticed Troy staring down at her. Their eyes met, hers melting into his penetrating gaze. His hand slipped out of hers and skimmed her waist. Rested on the small of her back. Pulled her closer.

"Were you dedicating that to me?" he murmured, his lips inches from hers.

"Of course I—"

A string of pitchy screams cracked through the air. Chloe lurched within Troy's embrace, her forehead bumping him in the mouth.

"Ouch!" he grunted.

"I'm so sorry! But did you hear that? It sounds like somebody is being attacked."

"Ahhh!"

The bloodcurdling scream ripped across the field, loud enough to eclipse the music.

"Yeah," Troy said, his head jerking in the opposite direction. "I hear it now."

Waves of people rolled in unison several yards away. A battle had erupted among the festivalgoers, bodies piling on top of bodies as fists pounded any moving target.

The crowd broke into a circle. Several roided-out men dressed in sleeveless crop tops and denim cutoffs wrangled in the middle. Bulging, veiny limbs became entangled, sending opponents slamming to the ground. Feet swung in the air and landed on the backs of those who'd succumbed to the beatings.

"Back up!" someone yelled. "He's got a knife!"

"A *knife*," someone else screeched. "I think I just saw a gun!"

Chloe and Troy charged the group as animalistic growls overrode the crowd's shouts. Insults were hurled. Several teenagers grabbed one another and spread out as a young man fell to his knees. He moaned, one hand clutching his side while the other sank into the mud. Spurts of bright red blood stained his white tank top.

Just as Troy set off to help him, he and Chloe were shoved to the side by security. The guards bum-rushed the crowd, a blur of neon-yellow windbreakers swooping in while attempting to break up the fight.

Flashes of metal swung through the air. The excruciating snap of cracking bones triggered sharp howls. Security became outnumbered. Concertgoers dived into a human dogpile, pouncing on one another like a rabid football team.

Troy made another attempt to go in.

"No!" Chloe insisted, holding him back right before Peyote Valley PD rolled up.

"Stand down!" they yelled with their weapons drawn.

The crowd gradually dispersed, exposing the damage that had been done. Several young men writhed in the dirt, clasping bloody wounds while groaning in pain. Police and security teamed up to make way for ambulances. Paramedics carrying stretchers forced their way into the circle.

As EMTs placed victims on gurneys, Chloe pulled Troy toward the exit. "We need to get to the police station. *Now*."

TROY HELD OPEN the door of Peyote Valley PD's headquarters and ushered Chloe inside. The precinct appeared more like a medical facility with its sterile white walls, dull gray floors and rows of plastic black-beam seating.

The pair approached the worn oak desk covered in Plexiglas.

"Hey!" a policewoman sporting a spiked blond Mohawk yelled from behind the slightly opened window. "You, in the New Edition T-shirt. Sit down!"

The scene around the station was chaotic, packed with festival attendees whose wrists were restrained with zip-tie handcuffs. Some were irate. Others were subdued. A majority of them appeared drunk, high or both.

Falling back down into her chair, the policewoman pointed up at Troy and Chloe. "What can I do for you two?"

"I'm Officer Troy Miller with the Maxwell PD," he told her, flashing his badge. "And this is my colleague Chloe Grant. We're here to find out exactly what went down at the Melodic Music Festival."

"Good to meet you. I'm Officer Nichols. Were you two there?"

"Yes, we were. And we saw some of what occurred when the riot broke out. But we couldn't make out much because it all happened so fast. All the distorted faces and fists flying… We'd be hard-pressed to identify anyone."

"Welp," she said, licking her finger before flipping open a report. "So far, six attendees have been rushed to the hospital. Two are being treated for stab wounds. One is in critical condition. Four suspects are being questioned as we speak."

"I'm sure you've heard about the Maxwell serial-killer investigation we're working on," Chloe said.

Leaning against the back of her worn mesh chair, the officer replied, "Ooh, yeah. I have. Sounds like a brutal case, from what I've read. Any leads on a suspect yet?"

"So far, no," Troy told her. "That's what brought us here to Peyote Valley. We think a couple of our victims attended the music festival in the past. So we were scoping out the scene, hoping to speak with some of the attendees or see if something might catch our attention. And I don't know if these two incidents are linked, but one of our victims was stabbed to death, and a knife fight broke out at the event."

"Hmm, interesting," Officer Nichols sighed while pulling at a stray chin hair.

"Do you think we could speak with one of the officers who's interviewing the suspects once they're done?"

"I'm sure that could be arranged. But judging by all the commotion around here, it might take a while. Not to mention, I don't think this attack has anything to do with your case."

"Why is that?" Chloe asked.

"Well, for starters, the guys who are being interrogated were charged with drug possession with intent to sell at *last* year's festival. So this isn't their first rodeo. They're all from California, and one of their fathers is a major politician. Thanks to Daddy's money and connections, they all got off with a stern warning. You'd think they would've learned their lesson. But *no*. They came right back this year and tried to pull the same stunt—"

The officer paused after screams echoed thorough the station.

"Hey, stop that!" a stocky policeman yelled as he shuffled over to two women and pulled them apart. "Take a seat. Both of you!"

Ignoring him, one of them yelled, "*You* brought those pills here, not me! This is on you!"

Her surgically enhanced breasts were practically spilling out of a tiny silver bikini top. The woman's cohort, whose floral crown was swinging from her long, tangled hair, responded by kneeing the woman in the stomach.

"Enough!" the officer grunted, grabbing them by the arms. "I'm locking both of you up."

"Ugh," Officer Nichols groaned, crossing her arms over her bulletproof vest. "It's gonna be a long night. But anyway, is there anything else I can help you two with?"

"There is," Chloe said. "Do you have any idea what brought on the knife attack?"

"I overheard a couple of officers saying the California dealers got a little too big for their britches. Stepped on the toes of some local drug dealers by trying to snatch up their clientele. They're lucky the firearms that were confiscated at the gate didn't make it inside."

"And I'm guessing most of these other people being detained are here on suspicion of illegal drug possession?"

"Majority of them, yes. But some are here for disorderly conduct, others for attempted robbery. You know how wild things can get at events of this magnitude."

"Got it," Troy said. "Excuse us for a second." He pulled Chloe to the side, disappointment tugging at his fallen expression. "So what are you thinking?"

"I think Officer Nichols is right. It doesn't sound like there's any connection between our killer and these stabbings. And judging by the look of things, we'll be here all night trying to speak with officers."

"Why don't I leave a business card for them, and if anything comes up they can give us a call?"

"Good idea. In the meantime, we can head back to Maxwell and see if there are any updates on the home front." No sooner were the words out of Chloe's mouth than their cell phones pinged simultaneously. "Speaking of an update, looks like we just got one."

"An email from Dani?" Troy asked.

"Yep. It was sent high priority. But not to the entire department. Just the two of us."

"Okay. Let's hear it."

Subject: PLEASE OPEN IMMEDIATELY
The victim we recovered from the Great Blue Heron Nature Preserve has been identified. Her name is Carla Eubanks. Chloe, she's connected to the dog tag that was

delivered to your house. Sergeant Donald Eubanks, the tag's owner who worked for the Chicago PD, was her father-in-law. Carla and her husband were living in Maxwell before her murder, but she grew up in Chicago.

On another note, Forensics ran DNA tests on the tag. Unfortunately no evidence was found. Let's meet once you two get back from the festival.

See you soon,

Dani

"So that's it," Chloe uttered, her mouth barely moving. "That's the connection. The killer's message keeps getting louder, Troy. He's going to greater lengths to get inside my head. How much longer until he actually gets to me?"

"We'll never know. Because I'm not going to let that happen."

Chapter Twenty-Three

Chloe jumped at the buzz of her cell, sending tomato sauce flying across the kitchen counter.

"You have *got* to calm down."

Seeing Dani's name on the screen brought a smile to her face. Chloe had never thought the day would come when they'd reconnect. While the circumstances surrounding their reunion weren't ideal, having her friend back felt amazing.

"Hey, D. What's going on?"

"I'm calling with some good news. *Finally.*"

"Well, I could certainly use some good news. Let's hear it."

"You know that partial fingerprint you lifted from the suitcase we recovered from the nature preserve? It contained twenty-two minutiae points."

"Meaning there are enough ridge structure changes to identify a suspect?"

"Possibly. The crime lab is in the process of running it through the FBI's Next Generation Identification system. So even if our suspect hasn't committed a crime, we could get a hit. Let's just hope his prints have been taken for licensing purposes or a background check."

Chloe closed her eyes, her hand trembling at the thought of getting a break in the case. "I hope this is it, Dani. I'm constantly on edge, just waiting for the other shoe to drop. That's no way to live. I left Chicago behind thinking my nightmare was over. And that Maxwell would be a safe space. But coming home has turned into a whole other ordeal."

"I know it feels that way. It won't for much longer, though. We're getting closer. I can feel it. I'm just glad we have you here. You've played a huge part in assisting us with this investigation."

"Yeah, well, none of this would be happening if it weren't for me—"

"Nope," Dani interrupted. "We're not about to do that. No passing the blame. Now, I called you with good news. So let's focus on it and hope something good comes of that fingerprint."

"You're right. I'll cut it out. Hey, on another note, I've got some news, too. It isn't as good as yours, but…"

"But what?"

"Chief Collins emailed me today. Hold on—I'll forward the message to you."

Subject: Good News and Bad News…
Hello Chloe,
I hope all is well. Great seeing you back in Chicago. It was a stark reminder of how much you're missed around here.

As promised, I did a little digging and came up with some info regarding Simon. The good news is he does in fact own a gun. A Smith & Wesson M&P 9mm, to be exact. But the bad news is he reported it missing over a month ago. So apparently it's been stolen.

I don't know whether or not that'll help your investigation, but it's all I got. I've attached a copy of the police report in case you need it. If anything else comes up, I'll let you know. Keep me posted on the case, and best of luck to you. Stay safe.

Sincerely,

Chief Collins

"Interesting," Dani said after several moments of silence. "Do you really think the gun was stolen? Or was this Simon's way of covering his ass in the event he *is* the killer and the weapon's traced back to him?"

"Option number two for sure. If Simon is the killer, which I totally believe he is, he's definitely lying about the theft so that he'll have an alibi."

"Well, he can run, but he can't hide from the truth. Between you and all of Maxwell PD, we'll find a way to unveil it. But for now, I'll file this message away in my high-priority folder in case we need that police report. In the meantime, when you talk to Troy, please tell him not to be mad at me for sharing the good news about the fingerprint with you before he did."

"I will. Speaking of Troy, what time are you gonna let him off work? I'm cooking his favorite dinner and would love to see him before bedtime."

"Wait—favorite dinner?"

"Yes. Smoky chipotle chicken chili, spicy sweet potato fries and skillet corn bread."

"Wait a minute. Are you and Troy a thing now?"

"Not officially, but we're getting there."

"Okay, then, *getting there*. I can hear that grin on your face all the way through the phone."

"Chief Miller!" Chloe heard someone call out. "You got a sec?"

"Be right there!" she replied before telling Chloe, "Listen, I've gotta run. But I'll try and let Troy off as soon as possible. You know we've got our hands full down here. I can't just rely on that fingerprint hitting in the database. The department is still swarming the streets in hopes of finding the suspect, too."

"Understood. Well, keep me posted on the print."

Just as the friends said their goodbyes, Chloe heard a light knocking at the door. Her first thought was that Troy had sneaked away from the station early. She shuffled through the living room and peered through the peephole, almost leaping into the air at the sight of her guest.

"Brody Rogers!" she yelled, throwing open the door. Chloe hadn't seen *The Chicago Force*'s head of security since her farewell gathering.

"Chlo-Chlo!" he shouted, a toothy smile spread across his entire face.

The moment she stepped onto the porch, the pair wrapped their arms around one another and held on tightly. Laying eyes on Brody's pleasantly familiar face felt therapeutic, reminding her that the time she'd spent in Chicago hadn't been all bad. He was one of the few people she'd trusted enough to share what she had been up to since leaving the city.

Chloe took a step back, eyeing Brody's freshly shaved head and thick muscles poking through his fitted black tracksuit. She wasn't used to seeing him dressed so casually. He'd always worn custom suits that fit his six-five physique to perfection, even while everyone else wore sweats and jeans.

"What are you doing out West?" she asked.

"Long story short, my security firm was hired to work on a big-budget movie that's filming in Phoenix. You know I couldn't come all this way without stopping by and saying hello."

"Well, I'm glad you did. Come on in. Let's catch up over, what? Water? Coffee? Wine? Meaning the whole bottle, considering all you've missed since I moved away."

"Ha!" Brody chuckled, following her into the living room. "Wine sounds good. But I'm going to pass and just have a glass of water."

"You must not be watching the national news."

"Not lately. What's going on?"

"We've got a serial killer here in Maxwell!" she called out from the kitchen.

"A *serial* killer? The way you used to talk about this place, I thought it was the safest town on earth."

Chloe came back with two glasses of water in hand and took a seat on the couch next to him. "Yeah, so did I. And it was, actually. Until I moved back. But anyway, I don't wanna talk about all that. I'd rather hear about you. How's your family? And how have things been around the set of *The Chicago Force*?"

"The family is doing well. Amy's holding down the fort back home and taking care of the kids while I'm out here. Filming is scheduled to wrap in another few weeks, so I won't be gone too much longer. Oh, Amy wanted me to tell you that she's listened to a few episodes of your podcast and loves it. What's the name of it again? *Prowler Among Us*?"

"No, *Preyed Upon*. I'm so glad to hear she's enjoying it. Have you had a chance to check it out?"

A shameful smirk broke out across Brody's face. "Honestly, no. Not yet, at least. The hours on this movie set are *long*. But trust me, I'll get to it. Can't wait."

"I'm gonna hold you to that."

"Please do. Oh, and as for *The Chicago Force*? I have nothing good to say. Things got really toxic after you left."

"Yeah, that's what I've heard. It's so hard to believe things could get any worse considering how tumultuous they were when I was there."

"Put it this way. Once you were gone, I lasted less than

a month. I ended up breaking my company's contract and getting the hell out of there. And I'll give you one guess as to who was instigating all the chaos."

Waving a hand in the air, Chloe quipped, "Well, it couldn't have possibly been Simon."

"Ha! See, that's what I miss. Your snappy sense of humor. We all missed it."

"Well, we did manage to have some fun times around the set. That is, when I wasn't being belittled for making sure the show's portrayals were accurate. I hope you know how much I appreciate the way you defended me against Simon."

Brody tossed his head back, downing his wine in one gulp. "No biggie. Who else was gonna step in on your behalf?"

"I never did understand why you were so loyal to me. The execs on that show were the ones signing your checks. Not me. But you didn't seem to care. It was almost as if my safety was your number one priority."

"You know, it was. One thing I can tell you about men is that we love to be needed. It's empowering. And intoxicating. Especially when it comes to a woman like you."

"What do you mean?" Chloe asked, her brows furrowing curiously as she set her glass down.

"What I mean is, you are a force. You're this commanding law enforcement officer who can obviously hold her own. Yet there's this other side of you that's kind and gentle. Not to mention beautiful. You're the perfect mix of what every man wants."

"Oh, I don't know about all that, but—"

"I'm strictly speaking for the men with good sense," Brody interjected. "Unlike that idiot ex-boyfriend of yours. *Alex Harrison.* I never did understand what you saw in that clown. And I still can't believe he let you get away."

"Trust me, I am filled with regret over that one. But he

didn't let me get away. I left him." Chloe hesitated as Brody inched closer toward her end of the couch. "I'm actually surprised you remember his name."

"I remember a lot of things. More than you can imagine. Blame it on my line of work. I have an ever-present desire to know more. To go deeper. Find out what makes people tick. I never was able to crack your shell and get inside that pretty little head of yours, though. Your guard's always been impenetrable. To the point where you seemed to think you were too good for me. Was that the case?"

"Of course not." Chloe's voice wavered as he brushed a few strands of hair away from her face. "I thought we'd developed a friendly rapport—"

"You're missing the point," Brody interrupted.

A long pause filled the space between them. He reached over and took her hand in his, holding it to his chest. Chloe's body stiffened as his erratic heartbeat pounded against her palm. His gaze, soft with sympathy just moments ago, had turned cold—his dark brown eyes darting around the room.

"Brody, are you okay?"

Silence.

"Brody," she repeated when his grip tightened. "Can you please let my hand go? You're hurting me."

"Am I?"

"Yes. You are."

A pang of nausea detonated inside Chloe's gut that snaked through her chest and up her throat. She attempted to pull her hand from his grasp. But he held on, his fingernails digging into her flesh.

Just as Chloe lurched forward, Brody pounced, a guttural snarl oozing through his chapped lips. He pushed her back down onto the couch and straddled her hips. His long, thick fingers clenched her neck. When she opened her mouth to scream, only a thin stream of air escaped her lips.

"Guess what, *Cece Speaks*?" Brody growled, spittle flying from his mouth. "You have no choice but to open up now. Because I've finally got you right where I want you. And this time, you're not getting away."

She clawed at his hands, wheezing, "Get off of me!"

"Aww, poor Chloe. You just don't get it, do you? This is it, sweetheart. You're done! I gave you chance after chance to *see* me. To want me. To reciprocate all that I'd done for you. Don't you know those *Chicago Force* executives wanted you outta there? And Simon wanted you dead! I saved you. But your snobby ass refused to give me a chance since I wasn't some hotshot attorney. And look at you now. Single, jobless, miserable and right back where you started. You're pathetic, you know that? No wonder the Chicago PD got rid of you. All that time on the force and you couldn't even figure out that I'm the Maxwell serial killer!"

Tears trickled down Chloe's temples as pressure filled her head. She pinched Brody's tanned, leathery skin while clutching his wrists, desperate to release his vise grip. But she couldn't. His hold was too strong.

"I just *knew* that upping the ante would finally get your attention," he rambled. "That you'd call on me after some maniac went on a killing spree in your hometown. Copying murders based on *your* podcast. I waited months to hear from you. Months! But I never did, you self-centered bitch. It's no surprise you thought some weak rookie cop could help you. You're pitiful, Chloe Lynn Grant. And that's why you're about to die."

No, she tried to scream, her throat constricting in his choke hold. Sweat dripped from Brody's forehead. Her lips tightened as she struggled to avoid the splashes of perspiration spraying her face.

"I should just shoot you," he grunted. "Right between the eyes. But I won't. That'll take all the fun out of squeezing your very last breath outta your body."

For a brief second, his grasp let up. Chloe didn't give him a chance to hunker back down before kneeing him in the groin.

"Aaah!"

She shoved him to the floor and jumped to her feet. Charging through the living room, Chloe threw open the console table drawer. Her gun wasn't there. She pivoted. Her purse was lying on the kitchen counter, the Glock's muzzle poking out.

Damn it!

Heavy footsteps pounded the teak floors. "Get your ass back here!"

Chloe ducked down behind the couch, then made a run for the kitchen. She slammed into the island, trembling while grabbing hold of her bag. Just as she rammed her hand inside, Brody approached. His fist struck her back, sending the purse flying across the room.

She bit down on her lip, fighting the pain before plunging an elbow into his chest.

"Bitch, you are *begging* me to kill you!" Brody fell against a bar stool and popped right back up. Flinging his body forward, he lunged in her direction.

Chloe raced toward the other side of the kitchen and dived for the knife block. She stumbled when Brody grabbed hold of her ankle. A swift kick to his head released his grip. She seized the eight-inch chef's knife and spun around, slicing his forearm in the process. Before she could go in for another cut, Brody flung his body against hers. They hit the floor in unison.

"Drop it!" he hollered, banging her wrist against the travertine tile.

Painful spasms shot up Chloe's spine. She writhed underneath his weight, her knuckles going numb as she refused to release the knife.

"I said, drop it!" Brody roared, the stench of cigarettes blowing from his mouth.

Chloe stabbed the floor while attempting to puncture his flesh. His legs thrashed from side to side as he skillfully avoided each blow.

"Don't make me mess up that pretty face of yours," he snarled. "Now gimme the damn knife!"

One final blow to her wrist sent the knife skidding across the floor. Tears of anger burned Chloe's eyes at the sight of it sliding underneath the refrigerator.

"Nooo!" she screamed, reaching up and ramming her thumbs into Brody's eyes. His sickening yelp irritated her eardrums. She ignored it, pushing even harder.

Bang!

Chloe's eyes widened at the sound of a gunshot.

"Get up!" someone yelled right before Brody was pulled to his feet.

She looked up. Rubbed the sweat and tears from her eyes. And saw Troy towering over them.

Sobs of relief shook her chest. As she struggled to stand, a piercing *crack* rose from the men's scuffle. Blood shot from Troy's nose.

Chloe willed her wobbly legs to carry her toward the island. While she scrambled for her purse, Troy thrust his gun against Brody's temple.

"I don't wanna have to shoot you!"

"Yeah, but I do," Chloe declared, aiming her gun at his chest. "And I will. Now stand down!"

Stumbling against the stove, Brody raised his hands in defeat.

"You got me," he muttered. "I'm done. You got me."

Just as Troy unholstered his handcuffs, Brody took a quick step forward and reached for them.

Bang!

"Damn it, Chloe!" Brody whimpered, clutching his right bicep. "You shot me!"

"And I'll shoot you again if you make another move."

He fell to his knees, then onto his side. The soles of his Timberland boots bounced against the floor, revealing what appeared to be spots of blood. A gun came clamoring out of his waistband. Troy kicked it out of his reach.

"Oh, so you really did have a gun on you this whole time?" Chloe asked, pulling his wrists behind his back while Troy cuffed him.

Brody replied with a moan, his eyes rolling into the back of his head.

"He threatened to shoot me," she told Troy, "but then changed his mind. Opted to strangle me instead so he could, and I quote, squeeze my very last breath from my body."

"My God…are you okay?"

Chloe took a deep breath. "Not yet. But I will be."

Epilogue

Troy tossed another log into the stone fireplace, then rejoined Chloe on the plush leather love seat.

"Mmm, thank you," he murmured after she handed him a pita cracker stacked with prosciutto and cheddar cheese.

The pair had rented out one of Cole's Ski Resort's most luxurious alpine-chic suites for the weekend. After all they'd been through, the much-needed getaway served as an opportunity to recharge away from the Maxwell-killer chatter.

Chloe rested her head against Troy's chest and pulled a faux mink blanket over them. Peering through the sliding glass doors, she stared out at the powdery aspen trees and majestic, snowcapped mountains. A long exhalation escaped her lips. She hadn't felt this tranquil, this alive, in a long time. Energy buzzed throughout her entire body as thoughts of the future filled her head. It was a sensation she'd never thought she'd feel again after her world had grown so dark. Solving the case was a huge feat. But it was Troy's love that brought her back to life.

"I'm so glad we decided to do this," he said, nuzzling her neck. "Being back here, together, feels surreal. It's like the ultimate full-circle moment."

"It really is. We spent so much time here as kids. Then, when I first moved back, this is where our first official date took place—"

"Oh?" Troy interrupted. "The day we went on that sleigh ride was an actual date?"

"Yes, it was. Or at least I thought so."

"Then why didn't it end with a kiss?"

"Because you didn't go in for one."

"Touché," Troy whispered before leaning in and caressing her lips with his. "Now, back to our full-circle moment. Since this investigation is finally behind us, it's nice to decompress right here with the woman I love."

"I couldn't agree more. You know what else is nice?"

"What's that?"

"The fact that we have your sister's blessing. And that she and I were able to rekindle our friendship."

"Oh, for sure. Dani's approval and you two reuniting has been the cherry on top…"

Troy's voice trailed off, his gaze shifting toward the private balcony.

"Hey," Chloe said, giving his chin a soft pinch. "What's wrong?"

"Nothing at all. I was just thinking about how happy I am with where we are. But I hate the way we got here. I mean, you went through hell back in Chicago, then returned to Maxwell and walked into an even worse situation—"

"Troy," she interrupted softly, running her hand along the back of his neck. "Let's not rehash the past. It's over. We both made it out alive. Brody is behind bars, and he's never getting out. You and I found our way back to one another. Maybe that rough road was the route we had to take in order for that to happen."

"You're right. And that road has made me all the more appreciative."

"Exactly."

Just as Chloe caressed his forehead with her lips, Troy's cell phone buzzed.

"Now, why is your phone going off? Didn't you tell everyone you're unavailable for the next few days?"

"I did. Maybe it's an emergency." He tapped the screen and let off a chuckle. "See, all that fussing you just did and this is the text we've been waiting on. The movers confirmed they'll be at my place next week Wednesday."

"Oh, good. You know, I already feel like you've been living at my place. But it'll be nice to make things official."

"It will be. But don't get too comfortable. This is just temporary. My Realtor is ready to start showing us places as soon as we are."

"What's your hurry?"

"There is no hurry. I'm just thinking about our future. You know, settling down, getting married, starting a family…"

"Hmm, I like the sound of—"

Bzzz…

"Oh!" Troy yelped, pointing at Chloe's phone. "Did *you* tell everyone you're unavailable for the next few days?"

"Of course I did! And I bet I can guess who's calling."

"Who? Maxwell PD's chief of police?"

"You got it," Chloe said before accepting the call. "Hey, Dani. I'm at the ski resort with your brother and you're on speaker, so watch what you say."

"First of all, please do not rub in my face the fact that you're spending a fabulous weekend at my favorite place with your man."

"Sorry, friend. Just know that our suite is hideous and we're having a *horrible* time."

"All lies!" Troy retorted. "Now, why are you disturbing us?"

"Pipe down, little brother. I won't keep you two. I'm actually calling with some good news. Chloe, that partial print you lifted from the suitcase got a hit in the national database."

"*Please* tell me it matched up with Brody's."

"It did."

"Yes!" Chloe exclaimed, jumping up from the couch. "We really needed that evidence. Especially after Brody claimed he never confessed to the murders the day he attacked me."

"Are you surprised? A lot of cold-blooded killers admit to their crimes, then recant their statements later. In this case, however, the amount of evidence is overwhelming. Brody admitted to having a personal vendetta against you. Then each of the murders mimicked episodes of your podcast to a T. But here's what you don't know. Jasmine Bailey's DNA was found on the soles of Brody's Timberland boots."

Pulling Chloe close, Troy whispered, "We got him, babe."

"Yes, we did."

Right before their lips met, Dani barked, "Hey! I can hear all that heavy breathing you're doing. Cut it out. At least until I hang up. Now, I've got one more piece of news to share, then I'll let you get back to your getaway. Ballistics came back on the firearm you two confiscated from Brody. The markings on the shell casing found with Carla Eubanks's body matched the weapon."

"That's great news," Troy said. "We were actually expecting it."

"Right. But were you expecting the serial number to match up with the gun that Simon Grazer reported missing?"

"Wait. *What?*" Chloe said as Troy's arms fell from her waist. "I—I'm sorry. But can you repeat that?"

"Brody somehow got ahold of the gun that Simon reported missing. My guess is that he stole it while they were on the set of *The Chicago Force*."

"And he thought he could frame Simon once his killing spree was over."

"Exactly."

"And you're sure about this?" Troy asked skeptically.

"Of course I'm sure! I compared the model and serial

number to Simon's police report. They both match up. Trust me. Everything checked out."

Grabbing Troy's arm to quiet him down, Chloe added, "I'm at a loss for words. I can't believe how this case had us stumped for so long. And now, finally, it's all coming together."

"Indeed it is," Dani agreed. "Now, look, I've held you two up long enough. If any new information comes in, I'll let you know. In the meantime, get back to your staycation. You both deserve this break and I'm sorry I interrupted it. But I just had to share that news."

"And we're glad you did," Chloe said. "Hey, one last thing. Be sure to check out the latest episode of *Preyed Upon* when you get a chance."

"Wait—you relaunched the podcast?"

"I did."

"Good for you! I'll definitely give it a listen. And with that, I'm hanging up. Talk soon."

When the call disconnected, Troy held Chloe closer. "Take a deep breath, babe. Take it all in. Be proud of your hard work and know that this win deserves a celebration. A *proper* celebration."

"Proper meaning what? Another champagne toast?"

"Um, no," he murmured, pulling her to her feet. "I was thinking of something a little more interactive. A vertical joyride, if you will."

"I think I know where you're going with this, and I like it." Chloe followed him into the bedroom, her head falling against his chest as he wrapped her in his arms. "Mmm, inside your embrace. My favorite place to be."

"And I hope you'll continue to feel that way. Always and forever."

* * * * *

Harlequin® Reader Service

Enjoyed your book?

Try the perfect subscription for Romance readers and get more great books like this delivered right to your door.

See why over 10+ million readers have tried Harlequin Reader Service.

Start with a Free Welcome Collection with free books and a gift—valued over $20.

Choose any series in print or ebook. See website for details and order today:

TryReaderService.com/subscriptions

RSBPA2409